THE DEAN'S DEVOTIONAL

21 PROVERBS FOR ACADEMIC LEADERSHIP

DR. DARYL D. GREEN

The Dean's Devotional

21 Proverbs for Academic Leadership

Dr. Daryl D. Green

WALK BY FAITH PUBLISHING
www.wbyf.site

The Dean's Devotional: 21 Proverbs for Academic Leadership

Author - Dr. Daryl D. Green

Front Photo image by Mr. Benjamin Baxter

Cover Design – Greta Kokalari

ISBN: 978-1-972760-00-0

Disclaimer
Some stories and situations in this book are based on the author's experiences in higher education leadership. In order to protect privacy, certain narratives are composites, and identifying details such as names, titles, dates, and locations have been changed or omitted. Any resemblance to specific individuals or institutions is unintended and purely coincidental. This book is offered for spiritual encouragement and general leadership reflection only and does not constitute legal, human resources, financial, or mental-health advice. Readers should seek appropriate professional counsel and follow applicable laws and institutional policies when making decisions.

Published in the United States by Walk By Faith Publishing, a division of Walk By Faith Worldwide. www.wbyf.site

For bulk orders, speaking engagements, or permissions, please visit www.darylgreen.org or email advice@darylgreen.org.

DEDICATION

To every academic dean who has ever gone home exhausted, wondering if the struggle is worth it

and to the students, faculty, and staff whose lives are quietly changed by your faithfulness.

And to my wife, Estraletta, whose love, prayers, and partnership have carried me through every season of leadership.

I also honor the legacy of the business school deans and leaders who served Langston University before me. Their vision, sacrifice, and commitment to excellence helped pave the way for the work I now carry forward. I stand on their shoulders with gratitude and responsibility.

"Dean's Devotional is a timely reminder that wisdom and faith can transform even the most challenging seasons of leadership. Dr. Green's reflections offer hope, clarity, and practical guidance for academic leaders navigating complexity with courage and grace. His journey demonstrates that obstacles are not endpoints but opportunities for renewal and growth. This resource will inspire leaders to lead with integrity, resilience, and vision. These are the qualities that strengthen both individuals and institutions."

— President Jackson
Langston University, 17th President

"A Dean's Devotional reflects the heart of a leader shaped by faith, perseverance, and calling. Since welcoming him to Oklahoma Baptist University in 2016, I have watched the Lord deepen and strengthen Dr. Green's leadership in higher education. His reflections offer wisdom, honesty, and spiritual encouragement for anyone serving in academic life. His book is a timely reminder that leadership is sacred work, and that God walks with us through every challenge."

— David W. Whitlock, Ph.D.
President, Southeastern Oklahoma State University

"In The Dean's Devotional, Dr. Daryl D. Green gives voice to the often unseen spiritual weight of academic leadership and reminds us that leadership in Christian higher education is a sacred calling. Drawing from Proverbs and shaped by the quiet, faithful work of rebuilding amid challenge, this devotional offers wisdom, courage, and clarity for leaders laboring to steward institutions and serve students well. This book will encourage deans and academic leaders to lead with faithfulness, perseverance, and trust in God's sustaining presence."

— Dr. Stan Norman
President, Williams Baptist University

"Dr. Daryl Green's The Dean's Devotional is a profound reflection of his mission to uplift higher education through a lens of faith, humility, and unwavering perseverance. By championing a selfless approach to collaborative scholarship, Dr. Green offers academic leaders an inspiring and essential blueprint for leading with heart and purpose."

— Professor Deborah M. Gaspard
2021-22 Board Chair, ACBSP
Metropolitan Community College

“Thisdevotionaloffersrareandneededinsight into the spiritual realitiesofacademicleadership.Drawingfrom real experiences in the dean’schair,Dr.Greenconnectsbiblicalwisdom to the daily decisions, pressures,andresponsibilitiesdeansface.Itis both a source of strength and a steadycompanionforleadersnavigatingcomplex seasons.”

—LauraDeLaCruz,Ed.D.,MBA,MPA, MS-HTRM
ACBSP Region #6 Chair,
Dean/Professor,AdvancedTechnologies,
Doña Ana Community College

“TheDean’sDevotionalisapowerful,personal, and profoundly useful resource.Dr.DarylD.Greenmasterfullyconnects biblical wisdom to modernhighereducationchallenges,offering a unique blend of spiritual guidance,administrativesmarts,andformation of a team that had a mind towork.Amust-readforthosewhowant to lead with integrity and purpose.”

— RobertLouisShepard,PhD
Author&Founder,TheShepardInstitute (TSI), LLC

“Asapastorandformeracademicadministrator, I understand the profoundresponsibilityandsacredtrustthat leadership entails. In the Dean’sDevotional,Dr.Greenremindsusthat effective leadership is sustainednotonlybysoundstrategybutbyintentional self-care and spiritualrenewal.TheDevotionalisatimely companion for leaders who seek to nurturetheirinnerlifewhilefaithfully navigating the complex and demandingcallingofacademicleadership.”

— Rev.Dr.JimmyArthurAtkins
TrueWorshipChristianFellowship,Cary, NC

"Dr. Daryl Green demonstrates that teaching and leading are more than a profession; they are a calling God placed on his life. His Christian faith shapes how he leads with humility, grace, patience, and perseverance. Dr. Green's servant's heart is evident in his consistent empowerment of others and in planting seeds for future growth."

— Dr. Xanshunta Polk
Associate Professor of Business & PMBA Program
Coordinator, King University

"The Dean's Devotional: 21 Proverbs for Academic Leadership is a book with powerful messages for those of us called to lead in higher education — particularly within the unique and sacred spaces of our beloved HBCUs. With honesty, grace, and wisdom, each chapter invites those of us in higher education to reflect not just on how we lead, but why we lead.

From the first chapter to the last, this devotional meets readers right where they are, and it reminds us that true leadership is rooted in boldness and faith.

I am deeply grateful to my fellow dean for this timely and necessary work."

— Dr. Tracy Harrell Dunn
Dean, Burroughs School of Business & Entrepreneurship,
Benedict College

TABLE OF CONTENTS

FOREWORD

As a pastor who has walked with leaders across the country, I have learned that the higher the office, the heavier the burden. Titles may change from pastor to president, chair to chancellor, dean to director, but the spiritual weight of leadership remains the same.

Academic deans bear a unique load. They stand in the crosscurrents of faculty expectations, student needs, financial pressures, and political realities that most people will never see. Their decisions quietly shape futures, families, and entire communities. Yet very few resources speak to the soul of the dean.

That is why this book matters.

My friend, Daryl D. Green, stepped into the deanship of Langston University's School of Business at a time when many would have turned away. The school had been without a full- time dean, morale was low, and the road ahead was steep. Instead of retreating, he prayed. Instead of leading by personality alone, he anchored himself in the wisdom of Proverbs.

What you hold in your hands is not theory; it is testimony. These twenty-one virtues are not abstract concepts pulled from a leadership seminar. They are the spiritual scaffolding that supported a real dean through real crises, accreditation pressures, personnel challenges, student needs, and personal health battles. Through it all, Dr. Green discovered that the role of a dean is not just strategic; it is spiritual.

As you read, you will be invited to do something rare in higher education: to slow down, to listen for God's voice, and to examine your own leadership in the light of scripture. Each devotional offers a proverb, a leadership focus, and a simple prompt to guide your decisions. This is a book you can keep on your desk, in your briefcase, or beside your Bible.

I believe that if more of our academic leaders led with this kind of wisdom, rooted in God's Word, honest about institutional realities, and humble enough to pray, we would see not only higher rankings, but more profound transformation in the lives of students and faculty.

To every dean, chair, provost, and academic leader who picks up this book: you are not alone. The same God who walked with Solomon in the palace and with Paul in the prison is ready to walk with you in the boardroom and the classroom.

May this devotional strengthen your heart, clarify your calling, and remind you that leadership in the academy is holy work.

Dr. M.L. Jemison, Senior Pastor

St. John Missionary Baptist Church

Oklahoma City, Oklahoma

ACKNOWLEDGMENTS

I thank God, the giver of wisdom, for sustaining me through the journey that birthed this book. Every chapter in these pages is a reminder that His grace is sufficient in the pressure cooker of academic leadership.

I must thank my wife of 36 years, Estraletta A. Green. You have walked with me through long nights, early mornings, and seasons when the chair felt too heavy. Your love has been my anchor.

To my children, Mario, Sharlita, and Demetrius, thank you for your patience, prayers, and honest feedback.

Special thanks to the dean's mentorship from Dr. Tracy Dunn, Dr. Donald Andrews, Dr. Marie Coleman, Dr. Jack McCann, Dr. David

Houghton, Dr. Michael Scott, Dr. Sherri Smith-Keys, Dr. Dorian Williams and Dr. Dan Reeder. I spent hours listening to their experiences and lessons learned. Their honesty, wisdom, and transparency helped me see around corners and prepared me for the realities of the dean's office. I was better prepared because they were generous with their stories.

I want to thank Caesar Andrews, Jr., my brother-in-law, for sharing his executive experience at Gannett and for offering practical insights on leading transformational change. His perspective helped me think more strategically about media, messaging, and institutional change.

I am also grateful to my former Department of Energy colleague, Terry Provost, a proud graduate of Prairie View A&M University. We met in Hanford in 1989. Terry quietly became one of my most important teachers since he championed managing millions of dollars in nuclear programs. His operational excellence, calm judgment, and wise counsel helped me navigate complex leadership challenges long before I ever sat in a dean's chair—much of how I think about systems, accountability, and stewardship was shaped by his example.

I want to especially thank President Ruth Ray Jackson, 17th President, Langston University, for giving me the incredible opportunity to serve as dean at such a historic and distinguished institution. The experience transformed me as a person as I navigated disruptive change, cultural resistance, and spiritual warfare.

I also want to thank President Heath Thomas at Oklahoma Baptist University for encouraging this move to Langston University and giving me his blessing to leave a dear institution that helped shape my calling. His support reminded me that the Kingdom is larger than any one campus.

I also thank Professor Brian Francis, whom I first hired as an adjunct because of his rich global experience, not yet knowing why our students, and I needed that exposure. I now call him "the Prophet of Langston." In a season of intense spiritual warfare, he quietly walked our hallways and prayed over our building when no one was watching; God knew I needed a prayer warrior like Professor Francis by my side.

To my pastoral and academic colleagues, mentors, and friends who encouraged me to tell this story, thank you.

To the faculty, staff, and students of the Langston University School of Business, you have been both my assignment and my inspiration. Your resilience, creativity, and grit have shown me what Proverbs looks like in real life.

Finally, to every reader who will pray through these pages and apply these truths, may the Lord multiply your impact in ways you cannot yet see.

ABOUT THE AUTHOR

Dr. Daryl D. Green,DSL, is a transformational business dean, leadership scholar, and change agent who has devoted his life to helping people lead with wisdom in uncertain times. Born and raised in Shreveport, Louisiana, he learned early the values of hard work, faith, and service from his parents
(Edward Elias and Annette Green Elias) and community.

Dr. Green earned a Bachelor of Science in Mechanical Engineering from Southern University, where he also met his wife, civil engineer Estraletta Andrews Green. He later completed a Master of Arts in Organizational Management from Tusculum College and a doctorate in Strategic Leadership from Regent University. His career spans more than three decades in both government and higher education. Before entering academia full-time, he managed more than 400 federal projects worth over $100 million for the U.S. Department of Energy by the age of thirty.

In higher education, Dr. Green served as the first Black business professor at Oklahoma Baptist University and now serves as Dean and Full Professor of the School of Business at Langston University, Oklahoma's only Historically Black College and University. At Langston, he has led a dramatic turnaround, growing enrollment, elevating national rankings, expanding corporate partnerships, and integrating AI and micro-credentials into business education. His students have scored in the top 1% nationally on the Peregrine Business Exam, and Langston's business school has risen into the top tier of HBCU programs.

Raised in a Christian home in the Cedar Grove community of Shreveport, Louisiana, Dr. Green's faith has been shaped through a lifetime of active service and discipleship. Over the decades, he has served faithfully in several churches, including First Baptist Church of Cedar Grove, Greater Faith Missionary Baptist Church in Pasco, Washington, Payne Avenue Missionary Baptist Church in Knoxville, Tennessee, and St. John Missionary Baptist Church in Oklahoma City. His ministry work has included leadership and service through the Christian Soldier Academy, tutoring programs, teaching, deacon service, marriage ministry, and dance and wellness initiatives. These experiences reflect a faith that has been practiced consistently over time through service, leadership, and care for others.

A prolific author, Dr. Green has written or co-authored more than fifty books, ebooks, and textbooks on leadership, small business, and personal growth. His insights have been featured in *USA Today, Ebony Magazine, BET, and the Associated Press.*

Together with his wife, he co-leads AGSM Consulting and the Mobile Dance Studio, mentoring leaders in boardrooms, churches, classrooms, and on the dance floor. Above all, Dr. Green is a man of faith who believes that to whom much is given, much is required.

PREFACE

When the Alarm Sounds and No One Moves

On one of my very first days as dean, the fire alarm went off. The sirens screamed. The lights flashed. The whole building pulsed with that urgent, mechanical voice that says, *Move now*.

But no one moved.

Classes continued. Faculty sat in their offices. Students glanced up, then went back to their screens. I stood in the hallway watching people work as if nothing were happening.

I mentioned it to a faculty member. He shrugged and said, "Oh, this is an old building. It's a false alarm."

I nodded politely, but everything in me tightened.

Before I was a dean, I was a safety engineer with the U.S. Department of Energy. In that world, you learn quickly: nothing good happens when you train people to ignore alarms.

A few weeks later, it happened again. The sirens blared. The lights flashed. This time, I didn't wait to see what anyone else would do.

I walked through the business school offices and said, "I'm leaving the building. If you decide to stay, I'll tell your family where to find your body."

I said it half in jest, but fully in earnest.

I must have shamed a few people, because they got up and followed. On my floor, most of the people evacuated. On the floors below, many stayed where they were. One attempted "solution" that surfaced later was to silence the audible alarms so classes wouldn't be interrupted.

That was a terrible idea.

Eventually, the fire system was repaired, and the alarms worked as they should. But the image stayed with me: a building full of intelligent people, sitting calmly under flashing lights, trained by history to believe that warnings did not matter.

Now imagine one more scene.

One day, there is not just a siren. There is *smoke*.

I see it first. I smell it in the hallway, curling under the office doors. I tell everyone, "There is smoke. There must be fire."

People look up, frown, and then look back down at their email. After all, it's *always* been a false alarm.

I keep calling for help to those on my floor and to those above me. Some are too busy. Some are too tired. Some are too invested in the story that "this building never actually burns."

That, in many ways, is what it felt like to become a dean.

The lights were already flashing when I arrived. Enrollment pressures. Accreditation warnings. Student complaints. Financial cliffs. Cultural dysfunction that everyone could feel but no one wanted to name. To many, these were just background noises, the way things had always been.

But I could smell the smoke.

I heard it in the students' stories. I saw it in the data. I felt it in the place's spiritual heaviness. I knew what could happen to a school that ignored its alarms. (Later, in the Conclusion, I will tell you about one that did.)

To be a dean on assignment from God is to live in that tension: between a blaring siren and a hallway full of people who have learned not to flinch.

It can be lonely. Some days you feel like a prophet crying in the wilderness while others sleep. You see where the structure is cracked. You know where the gates are burned. You see where the people are vulnerable. And you know, deep in your spirit, that pretending everything is fine will not save anyone.

This devotional was born in that space.

It was written in the long days and late nights of rebuilding a business school that many had quietly written off. It was shaped by eighteen months in which God took what some called "the worst organization on campus" and, through much prayer and painful change, turned it into a story of turnaround and hope.

Each chapter reflects on a virtue from Proverbs: wisdom, discernment, courage, humility, generosity, and more and ties it to real moments from my life as a dean: meetings that went sideways, students on the brink, faculty at cross-purposes, budgets that didn't add up, and miracles that did.

I do not offer myself as a perfect example. I offer myself as a fellow traveler who has heard both the sirens and the silence, and who has learned that leadership in the academy is not just strategic work; it is spiritual work.

I had managed hundreds of federal projects worth millions of dollars. I had worked in complex, high-stakes environments. But nothing felt like this: a school seen by some as 'the biggest liability at the university,' low morale, broken trust, students who had quietly lost hope, and a system that seemed designed for burnout rather than flourishing.

That night, I did what Nehemiah did. I prayed.

Nehemiah heard about the broken walls of Jerusalem and the vulnerable people living inside them. He wasn't a priest or prophet, he was a cupbearer, a trusted servant working inside a foreign system. He wept. He fasted. He prayed. And then he asked for permission and resources to rebuild.

As I stepped into the dean's role at Langston University, I realized I wasn't just managing budgets and schedules. I was walking into a city with broken walls: students discouraged, faculty divided, systems fractured, and trust eroded. In many ways, I had accepted a Nehemiah assignment without fully realizing it.

The more I listened to our students, the more clearly, I understood the stakes. *To protect the privacy of students, faculty, and colleagues, many of the stories in this book are composites, and some identifying details have been changed.*

Over the next 18 months, God began to move in ways that reminded me of Nehemiah's wall.

Faculty who had once checked out started showing up. Students who had given up on the school began to believe again. National rankings shifted. Enrollment grew. Accreditation concerns turned into opportunities for reform. We didn't rebuild "in 52 days" like Nehemiah, but the transformation was just as miraculous to me because I knew where we started.

If you're an academic dean, you know the weight of the chair. You inherit decisions you didn't make, budgets you didn't design, cultures you didn't create, and crises you didn't start. You are asked to protect the institution, serve the students, support the faculty, satisfy accreditors, reassure parents, and calm presidents and provosts often in the same week.

You live in what I call the *New Normal*:

- shrinking resources and rising
- expectations, enrollment cliffs and escalating
- compliance, disruptive technologies and fragile
- human beings, public scrutiny and private pain.

And yet…God has trusted you with this season.

This book is my attempt to walk beside you as a fellow dean, not as a superhuman leader. I have cried out for help in my office. I have considered resigning. I have wrestled with personnel decisions that kept me up at night. I have felt misunderstood, misjudged, and at times unseen.

But I have also seen God's faithfulness in small miracles, changed hearts, restored programs, and students whose lives were turned around because someone in a dean's office chose to lead with wisdom instead of fear.

And because philanthropy is now part of my obedience, I want you to know this: Most of the proceeds from this book will be returned directly to this mission of educating students.

If you have ever smelled smoke in your institution and wondered if anyone else noticed…

If you have ever walked your campus feeling like the only one who believed the alarms…

If you have ever asked God, "Why did You send me into this building at this time?"

Then this book is for you.

INTRODUCTION

No one prepares you for the spiritual weight of being a dean. You are expected to lead with clarity while navigating constant pressure, competing expectations, and decisions that rarely have clean answers. In those moments, leadership is not just strategic. Leadership is deeply personal and, at times, profoundly spiritual. This book was born in those moments.

Three Orders, One Calling, and a Wall to Rebuild

What gets measured gets done! Before I started as dean, the Vice President of Academic Affairs gave me three clear performance metrics for this dean job:

1. *Show up to work.*
2. *Let the students see you.*
3. *Let the faculty know who's in charge.*

I smiled and nodded. It sounded straightforward. On paper, it sounded simple, almost too simple.

Important Context for the Reader

The experiences reflected in this book are not unique to Langston University or to HBCUs. Over many years of service in higher education, including participation in accreditation site visits and conversations with deans, presidents, and vice presidents across the country, I have consistently encountered similar organizational challenges—low faculty morale, advising breakdowns, leadership turnover, resource constraints, and institutional cultures resistant to change. These realities are not confined to one campus or one sector of higher education. Rather, they represent common pressures faced by academic leaders nationwide. The reflections in this devotional are therefore intended to speak to the universal challenges of academic leadership, offering wisdom and encouragement that extend well beyond any single institution.

Not long after, another administrator made a comment that stopped me in my tracks: "The business school office is often dark."

Students confirmed it in their own way. More than one said quietly, "Dean, I've never even seen your business office before." They weren't talking about me personally. They were describing the culture they had grown used to: a dark office, a closed door, an invisible leadership presence.

I made a decision: if God had placed me in this chair, I was going to bring light, physically and spiritually. I literally turned on the lights in the office suite and kept my door open. I quickly established an open-door policy for students, faculty, staff, and anyone who needed to talk. If you walked down the hallway, you would see me there, present. I wanted students to know: *There is someone in this office for you.*

At the same time, I was stepping into a paradox.

Many of our students were living on campus and paying dormitory fees, yet the majority of their classes were online. Faculty were working from home. Lecture halls sat empty while student complaints filled my inbox. As I later learned, this was not laziness. It was a symptom of faculty shortages. One faculty member was carrying as many as 10 courses in a semester, when a normal full-time load would have been four or five.

Now imagine being the dean tasked with explaining to parents why their children were paying for an on-campus experience but rarely seeing a professor in a classroom. They didn't want a spreadsheet. They didn't want to hear excuses. They wanted a shepherd.

I had many problems to fix. I knew immediately that "showing up" would require more than parking in a reserved spot. It would mean confronting systems, mindsets, and habits that had gone unchallenged for years. Before I tried to change anything, I did the only wise thing I knew to do:

I asked God for strength on this journey.

Watching, Fighting, Building

Within my first 18 months, I faced more HR issues than many deans see in a decade: difficult personnel decisions, reassignments, non-performance, and a constant stream of crises that never showed up in the job description. One employee stopped showing up to work. Others showed up physically but not mentally or spiritually. Faculty morale was low. Trust from the upper administration was fragile. Students were frustrated and, in some cases, traumatized by past experiences.

I began to frame my work as a dean through the lens of Nehemiah. When Nehemiah returned to Jerusalem, he did three things at once:

He watched. He walked the walls at night, carefully assessing the damage others ignored.

He fought. He confronted enemies, managed internal conflict, and refused to be intimidated.

He built. He organized the people, assigned clear roles, and kept them focused on the work.

That became my mental model for the dean's office:

- Watch – Pay attention to data, culture, student stories, and unspoken tensions.
- Fight – Stand up for what's right, even when it's unpopular. Protect your people and your mission. Share our success stories, whether online or in person.
- Build – Create systems, programs, partnerships, and opportunities that outlive your tenure.

As I walked those "walls" at Langston University, listening to students, reading reports, walking through darkened hallways, turning on lights one switch at a time, God kept bringing me back to the book of Proverbs.

I discovered something crucial: Spiritual leadership is not separate from academic leadership. It is the engine of it.

From "Worst Organization" to a Wall Rebuilt

When I arrived, the School of Business had been described as "the worst organization on campus" with the most student complaints, conditional reaffirmation from ACBSP, only about 270 students, and poor graduation and retention rates. Eighteen months later, by God's grace, enrollment had grown past 400 students, seniors ranked in the top 1% nationally on the Peregrine Business Exam, and we were recognized as a top 30 HBCU business school and one of the Best HBCUs for Entrepreneurship.

Why a Devotional for Deans?

Most leadership resources for deans focus on strategy, finance, governance, or accreditation. Those are essential. But very few books look you in the eye and ask:

- How is your soul as you chair another meeting?
- Where do you go with the fear you won't say out loud?
- How do you navigate criticism without becoming cynical?
- Who shepherds the shepherds of the academy?

As a dean, you live in a world of dashboards and data, retention rates, credit hour production, faculty load, budget variance, rankings, and exam scores. I celebrate numbers because they represent real lives. But behind every metric is a leader who is either grounded or drifting.

This devotional is not another performance metric. It is an invitation to anchor your leadership in Proverbs, letting God's wisdom shape your decisions, tone, boundaries, courage, and even your generosity.

Each of the 21 chapters centers on:

- A Virtue drawn from Proverbs (wisdom, discernment, integrity, courage, and more).
- A scripture you can carry into your day.
- A Dean's Reflection grounded in real academic life.
- A Brief Application to connect scripture to your campus realities.
- A Leadership Prompt to help you pray, journal, or plan your next step.

The majority of the proceeds from this book will help establish an endowed fund at Langston University to support student retention scholarships and faculty development. In other words, these pages are not just about your soul; they are also about keeping students in school and helping faculty grow.

If the chair has ever felt too heavy...
If you've ever wondered if it's worth it...
If you've ever felt alone in the role...

This devotional is for you.

May God meet you in these pages the way He met me in the dark hallways and the lit offices, in the chaos and the quiet, and in the daily work of rebuilding.

CHAPTER 1 - WISDOM

Theme: Wisdom in the Hot Seat

Scripture – Proverbs 4:7
"Wisdom is the principal thing; therefore, get wisdom: and with all thy getting get understanding."

Dean's Reflection

I entered the dean's seat believing I was ready, 27 years of federal leadership experience, strategic plans memorized, and a reputation for staying calm under pressure. But on Day 1, my assistant informed me she would be gone for weeks. Suddenly, I was alone. Students were in crisis. A faculty member rushed in, nearly panicked, trying to manage ten classes at once. I had no roadmap, no policies, and no mentorship. I had to lean on wisdom beyond my own.

That night, I got on my knees and asked God to direct my path, and He did. Not through flashy miracles, but through wise counsel from other deans and divine insights at moments when I had nothing left to give.

Application for Academic Leaders

In moments of chaos, pause. Seek wisdom in scripture, from trusted mentors, and through quiet reflection. Don't rush to react; respond with discernment.

Leadership Prompt

What is one difficult decision you made that required more wisdom than knowledge, and how did you grow from it?

CHAPTER 2 – DISCERNMENT

Theme: Reading Between the Lines

Scripture – Proverbs 18:15
"The heart of the prudent getteth knowledge; and the ear of the wise seeketh knowledge."

Dean's Reflection

When I arrived at Langston, I promised myself that I would spend the first year on a listening tour before making hasty decisions. Wise leaders do not make significant changes on day one. They walk the walls first.

So, I listened.

I met with students, faculty, staff, and administrators. I read reports. I asked questions. And a pattern began to emerge: students were frustrated, confused, and, in some cases, deeply hurt by prior experiences. Complaints about advising, faculty availability, communication, and fairness were not isolated; they were consistent.

Meanwhile, the key leaders in the organization were singing a very different song:

"Everything is great."

"If it isn't broke, don't fix it."

"You can't trust students; they complain about everything."

One of them spent hours trying to persuade me that what I was seeing and hearing "did not happen." According to their narrative, the issue was my perception, not the reality in front of us.

That placed me at a crossroads:

Would I trust the soothing voices telling me to relax, or the uncomfortable evidence and student stories that refused to disappear?

In prayer, God gave me discernment. I realized these individuals were not merely offering another perspective; they were attempting to convince me of a lie. My responsibility was not to protect their version of reality. My responsibility was to seek the truth.

Discernment meant:

- Giving careful weight to students' voices and lived experiences.
- Observing patterns in complaints, without dismissing them as mere noise.
- Listening attentively to faculty and staff whose experiences align with students' accounts.
- Understanding that "everything is fine" can sometimes be a warning, not reassurance.

God showed me that there were real problems that needed to be addressed. To ignore them would not be wisdom, but negligence.

In closing, discernment is crucial for a dean, because you sit at the intersection of many competing stories. Some people will try to minimize problems while others will exaggerate them. Your calling is not to follow the loudest voice, but to seek the Lord's voice and the truth that lies beneath the surface.

Application for Academic Leaders

Discernment shields your campus from both denial and panic.

- Listen long before you decide. Conduct your own "listening tour" and record diligently what you hear.
- Refuse to be led astray by convenience. When influential voices say, "There is nothing to see here," yet the data and students testify otherwise, pause and pray.
- Triangulate reality. Compare student complaints, faculty feedback, and administrative reports. Note where they align and where they diverge.
- Ask God for clarity. Proverbs teaches that the ears of the wise "seek out" knowledge; therefore, do not wait passively, but seek actively.

Leadership Prompt

Where are you currently hearing mixed messages about a program, a person, or a process? Take one situation this week and deliberately:

1. Seek at least two additional perspectives.
2. Pray earnestly for discernment before making your next decision.

Write down what God shows you.

CHAPTER 3 – INTEGRITY

Theme: The Line You Will Not Cross

> *Scripture – Proverbs 11:3*
> "The integrity of the upright shall guide them: but the perverseness of transgressors shall destroy them."

Dean's Reflection

Before becoming a dean, I was deeply involved with our accreditation agency, ACBSP. I served first as a site-visit team member and later as a team leader. Those experiences profoundly shaped my understanding of integrity.

On one visit, our team was assigned to a business school that had undergone massive changes just before our arrival: new leadership, new programs, and new processes. Accreditation headquarters had gently suggested that the school delay the visit until things settled down. Instead, they pressed forward.

When we arrived, the administration's story was confident:

"Everything is implemented."

"All the new systems are up and running."

"Students are already benefiting."

Yet, as we investigated further, the evidence did not match the narrative.

Policies were written but not followed.

New structures were announced, but they were not truly functioning.

We were not there to embarrass anyone; we were there to verify. Still, the pressure was real: it would have been far easier to accept the assurances, write a glowing report, and move on, no conflict, no pushback, no hard conversations.

That was where integrity drew a line in the sand.

As team leader, I bore a responsibility to my accreditation body, to future students, and to every other honest institution in the pipeline. Our team reported only what we could verify, not merely what we were told. We documented the gaps between claims and reality to assist the Commissioners in making a fair and informed decision.

It was neither comfortable nor popular, but it was right.

That moment marked my emergence as a dean. I realized that:

- Integrity in accreditation signifies placing facts above feelings.
- Integrity in leadership entails refusing to allow fear, politics, or convenience to shape the narrative.
- Integrity in my own school requires that I be as honest concerning our weaknesses as I am proud of our strengths.

If we desire our students to walk in integrity, they must see it exemplified in us, especially when the stakes are high.

Application for Academic Leaders

Integrity is your internal compass when pressure tries to bend your judgment.

Speak the truth in reports and meetings, even if it delays approval or invites scrutiny.

- Resist the urge to over-promise regarding what your school has "already implemented." Be transparent about what remains in progress.
- Safeguard the credibility of your institution by declining to endorse numbers, narratives, or policies you cannot, in good conscience, defend.
- Remember, integrity fosters long-term trust. Administrators, accreditors, faculty, and students may not always welcome your reports, but they will come to recognize your trustworthiness.

Leadership Prompt

Think of a recent situation in which telling the whole truth seemed costly, whether in terms of data, outcomes, or capacity. How did you respond?

What is one area in your life right now where you need to strengthen your integrity, so that your "yes" and "no" are fully honest before God?

CHAPTER 4 – PATIENCE

Theme: Slow Work, Strong Foundations

Scripture – Proverbs 14:29
"He that is slow to wrath is of great understanding: but he that is hasty of spirit exalteth folly."

Dean's Reflection

In higher education, we often speak of "student transformation," yet we frequently forget that transformation is messy in the middle.

Early in my time at Langston, I met a freshman covered in tattoos and adorned with multiple piercings. He entered our space with a confident swagger, a look that some might hastily label "unprofessional."

One staff member became fixated on a certain student's appearance.

"Dean, that's not professional."

"He should remove those piercings."

"He doesn't look like business material."

Her concern focused on how he looked, not who he could become.

But when I looked at him, I saw something different: potential.

I saw curiosity.

I saw energy.

I saw someone who needed direction, not condemnation.

Behind the scenes, I began to mentor him, not with a spotlight or an official program, but with quiet, consistent guidance.

We talked about classes.

We talked about discipline.

We talked about choices and consequences.

We talked about who he wanted to be in four years, not just what he looked like as a working professional.

He was not the only one. Over time, I had the privilege of advising many first-year students who seemed "wild," unfocused, or undisciplined. On the surface, they didn't always fit the picture of a polished business professional. But beneath the tattoos, hoodies, piercings, and attitudes were young adults in process, some first-generation, some carrying heavy trauma, all striving to figure out life.

Four years later, that same student, who had drawn so much criticism, no longer looked like the caricature some had created.

- He had matured.

- He had grown in confidence and purpose.
- He had learned to navigate professional spaces without losing his identity.

God had transformed that student, not overnight, but gradually over time.

That is when patience becomes a spiritual discipline for deans and faculty. We must:

- Resist the temptation to judge the futures of students by their appearance in their freshman year.
- Remember, we ourselves are not yet finished works.
- Show the same measure of grace and patience that God has granted unto us.

In faculty and staff meetings, I often remind our people: "Be kind to your students. Give them space to grow, and do not judge them too quickly by what you see today."

We are called to be stewards of potential, not keepers of perfection.

Patience is not passivity. It is not the ignoring of misconduct, nor the lowering of standards. Rather, it is holding to standards while holding space: space for growth, repentance, development, and change.

If we desire testimonies of transformation at graduation, we must first exercise patience in their freshman year.

Application for Academic Leaders

Patience is seeing students through a long lens.

- Look beyond the surface. Tattoos, piercings, slang, or shaky study habits are but snapshots, not the final portrait.
- Invest in the "messy middle." Quiet mentoring, minor corrections, and consistent encouragement often bear more fruit than a single, dramatic intervention.
- Coach your team to slow their judgments. When faculty or staff complain about appearances or attitude, gently redirect them to ask: "Where might this student be in four years with the right support?"
- Remember your own journey. Most of us would not wish to be permanently judged by our eighteen-year-old selves.

Patience keeps you from giving up on students God is not finished with yet.

Reflection Questions

1. Think of a student who once seemed "too much" or "too far gone" but later surprised you. What helped them grow?
2. Where are you most tempted to judge students quickly: their appearance, communication style, attendance, or attitude?
3. How might your school's culture change if faculty and staff viewed freshmen as raw material rather than finished products?

Leadership Prompt

This week, choose one student who seems rough around the edges, someone others may dismiss.

- Pray for them by name.
- Initiate one intentional conversation: ask about their story, their goals, and their challenges.
- Ask God to give you patient eyes to see who they can become, not just who they appear to be right now.

Then, model that patience in how you speak about students in every meeting and email.

CHAPTER 5 – PURPOSE

Theme: Lead with Intent

Scripture – Proverbs 19:21
"There are many devices in a man's heart; nevertheless the counsel of the Lord, that shall stand."

Dean's Reflection

"How do you lead as a dean without a purpose-driven life?" Problems appear endless. Purpose shapes the direction of leadership. This virtue sharpens intent, steadies decisions, and gives meaning to the work when the demands of academic life feel overwhelming. Without purpose, the deanship becomes a cycle of tasks. With purpose, the role becomes a calling.

I witnessed the power of purpose firsthand during the 2024 ACBSP Leadership Symposium where I co-presented with Dean Tracy Harrell Dunn of Benedict College—one of the most accomplished deans in the HBCU community. After nearly two decades of service, she became the first woman to lead the Tyrone Adam Burroughs School of Business and Entrepreneurship and the fourth dean in its history.

Her presentation included a slide so full of accomplishments that I stared at it in admiration, including #1 SC HBCU Business School in Innovation & Entrepreneurship. Her business school record was impressive. As she completed that stunning overview, Dean Dunn paused and shared a statement that will stay with me forever:

"Just think what we could have accomplished if I had more buy-in from all faculty."

The room fell quiet. That sentence revealed a truth every dean eventually learns: even the most capable leader cannot succeed without resistance, setbacks, and incomplete cooperation. Yet, Tracy's purpose never wavered. Her purpose fueled every accomplishment on that slide. Her purpose drove the innovation, the programs, the partnerships, and the transformation that shaped Benedict College's business school into a national model.

Purpose was her engine.

When I stepped into my own deanship, I carried hopes, plans, and dreams for Langston University's School of Business. But like many new leaders, I quickly learned that plans alone do not carry you through the challenges. Purpose does. The leadership insights we shared in our presentation about identity, transitions, culture, and sustaining success reminded me that a leader must know *why* they are called into the role.

Purpose helps the dean endure long hours, difficult conversations, shifting campus dynamics, accreditation pressure, and cultural battles.

Purpose helps you stand tall when criticism stings or when progress feels slow. Purpose helps you push forward when the institutional climb is steep.

Scripture reminds us that although we may craft many plans, "the counsel of the Lord... shall stand." God's purpose, not human preference, establishes the work of the dean. When a leader aligns with divine purpose, the assignment becomes blessed, strengthened, and sustained. Purpose carries leaders through every season, from resistance to renewal.

And when purpose guides you, the institution God entrusted to your care becomes fertile ground for transformation.

Application for Academic Leaders

What is the deeper calling behind your leadership? Consider Dean Dunn's example. Her purpose carried her far beyond the limitations she faced. What might God do in your school if you lead, not from pressure, but from intent?

- Revisit your job description and prayerfully ask: What is the deeper calling behind my leadership?
- Where am I leading mostly from obligation or habit, and where am I leading from a God-given intent to serve students and protect the institution?
- Identify one decision this week where you will consciously lead not from fear or routine, but from holy intent.

Leadership Prompt

Ask yourself throughout the week:

"Am I leading with intent?"

Purpose-driven leadership doesn't just move institutions forward. It transforms them.

CHAPTER 6 – HUMILITY

Theme: Leading from the Back of the Line

> *Scripture – Proverbs 22:4*
> "By humility and the fear of the Lord are riches, and honor, and life."

Dean's Reflection

My first semester as dean was filled with speaking tours, listening sessions, and countless attempts to understand the true pulse of campus life. I made a deliberate choice early on: reach the students first. If the business school was to lead, then I needed to hear directly from the young people we were entrusted to serve.

As I observed campus leadership, something caught my attention. Many of the recognized student leaders- organization presidents, ambassadors, and influencers—were business majors. That gave me hope... but not confidence. Not yet.

Then the Student Government Association president, a business major himself, requested a meeting. We sat down for what I assumed would be a warm welcome and a quick overview of student life.

But God had a different lesson in store.

He spoke openly about academic advisement issues, faculty availability, and communication gaps. He was careful, diplomatic—too diplomatic. So, I pressed him gently: "If you had to grade our business school, what grade would you give us?"

He hesitated. I pressed again.

He exhaled and said quietly:

"Dean... I would give the business school a D."

I thanked him.

He looked surprised. But I was raised by parents (Edward Lee Elias and Annette Green Elias) who taught me that truth, even painful truth, is a gift. My mother believed in telling the whole story, and my father believed in accountability. Their lessons trained me never to run from reality. Humility doesn't resist truth. It receives it. Everyone seems to love the title "Dean." The job is bigger than the title, however.

I still felt compelled to hear from more students. So I requested an opportunity to speak before the entire SGA Senate. I wanted to introduce myself, hear their concerns, and share my commitment to build a student-centered business school.

I asked for questions.

But I received something else.

A senator stood up, looked me directly in the eye, and said with conviction: "Dean Green, the business school is a 3 out of 10."

The room grew still.

Then something happened that felt like a scene straight out of a Baptist church testimony service. A graduating senior, an accounting major I knew well, stood and declared: "I agree!"

In that moment, her agreement felt like a resounding "Amen, sister!" echoing through the sanctuary.

I stood there humbled. Not humiliated—humbled.

Because if the school earned a D, then I earned one too.

I was the dean of a D business school.

Some leaders defend, deflect, and deny. But my upbringing didn't allow me that luxury. I learned early that you cannot fix what you refuse to face. And humility is the doorway to transformation. Pride keeps leaders blind; humility keeps leaders teachable.

This truth is echoed in a saying I have always cherished:

"The most dangerous king is the king who believes the crown proves he is wise."

Titles deceive.

Corner offices deceive.

Praise deceives.

Nothing blinds a dean faster than believing the role is evidence of greatness. Leadership positions reveal character. They do not replace it.

After that meeting, I prayed harder, listened longer, and worked deeper. I reminded myself: "A D is not my destiny, but it is my starting point." The student feedback did not diminish my calling; it clarified my assignment.

The turnaround we later achieved—enrollment growth, accreditation strength, national exam performance, alumni re- engagement—did not come from ego. It began at the altar of humility.

Academic leaders often fight battles of pride:

- Prestige of title
- Proximity to presidents
- Board recognition
- Faculty politics
- Status in the accreditation community

But scripture warns us plainly:

"A man's pride shall bring him low."

In higher education, pride doesn't just bring leaders low. It drags entire units down with them. Prideful deans defend broken systems. Prideful deans ignore student voices. Prideful deans worship reputation instead of responsibility. And prideful deans forget that leadership is stewardship, not self-promotion.

Humility, however, builds legacy.

Humility invites growth.

Humility hears truth, even when truth stings.

Humility transforms leaders and the institutions God entrusts to them.

I thank God for the students who gave me that D.

They didn't insult me—they instructed me.

They didn't shame me—they sharpened me.

They didn't disrespect me—they directed me.

Without humility, I might have led from assumption instead of awareness. With humility, I could finally begin the work God called me to do.

Application for Academic Leaders

- Humility in academic leadership is not soft. It is a steel- covered towel.
- It frees you to do what needs to be done instead of what looks impressive.
- It keeps you close to your students, staff, and adjuncts instead of floating above them. It reminds you that God can use a broom, a van, and a title with equal power if your heart stays low and your hands stay ready.

You do not lose authority by serving; you gain credibility. The campus may respect your title, but they will remember your humility.

Leadership Prompt

Ask yourself daily:

"Am I leading from pride—or from humility?"

Humility is not weakness.

Humility is wisdomwrapped in strength.

CHAPTER 7 - KINDNESS

Theme: The Power of a Gentle Word

Scripture – Proverbs 3:3–4
"Let not mercy and truth forsake thee: bind them about thy neck; write them upon the table of thine heart: so shalt thou find favor and good understanding in the sight of God and man."

Dean's Reflection

I've learned that kindness isn't merely a virtue; it is a leadership strategy. At Langston University School of Business, we host Donuts with the Dean every second Tuesday of the month. On the surface, it may seem like just coffee and donuts, but it is far more than that. It is a community. It is healing. It is hope.

I remember our first gathering. Students arrived shyly at first, but the warm glaze of donuts and genuine conversation softened barriers. Faculty trickled in. Staff joined. The aroma of fresh coffee mingled with laughter. We were creating a space where everyone felt seen. Kind acts cultivate opportunities.

Consider this scenario: one day, a student quietly approached me and said, "Dean Green, I almost dropped out last semester. But I came to Donuts with the Dean, and you remembered my name. You asked how I was doing, and that changed everything for me."

Moments like that remind me that kindness costs little but pays immeasurable dividends.

In a high-pressure environment like academia, kindness is often the first casualty. Yet I have learned to slow down, greet others by name, offer encouragement, and treat everyone with dignity, whether a first-year student or a faculty member who has lost their way.

Application for Academic Leaders

- Host regular informal events (like "Donuts with the Dean") to create safe spaces for engagement.
- Practice *name-based leadership*, learn and use the names of students, staff, and faculty.
- Acknowledge others publicly, and correct privately.
- Model kindness in faculty meetings, even during disagreements.
- Empower your admin team to mirror your tone of gentleness.

Leadership Prompt

- Who in your college needs a gentle word today?
- What small act of kindness could create a ripple effect across your school?

CHAPTER 8 – TEACHABILITY

Theme: When the Dean Becomes the Student

Scripture – Proverbs 9:9
"Give instruction to a wise man, and he shall be yet wiser: teach a just man, and he shall increase in learning."

Dean's Reflection

Academic leadership will break your heart if you allow it.

As a dean, I have witnessed what the pressure of this work can do:

- Marriages quietly fall apart.
- Health declines from "a little stress" to a severe medical crisis.
- Friendships and professional relationships crumble under politics, ego, and exhaustion.

There were mornings when I woke up and my blood pressure was already sitting around 160/100. Before I even reached the office, my body was telling the truth about my stress. I had no idea what the day would bring, who would show up for work, or what crisis or conflict would be waiting in my inbox.

In that season, I could have become harder, colder, and more controlling. Many leaders do. Instead, God used my wife, Estraletta, to invite me into something different: teachability.

Estraletta was intentional about us reconnecting, not just as ministry partners or co-laborers in life, but as husband and wife. She got us back into ballroom dancing. I am convinced this was the Lord's curriculum for my soul.

Without asking for my permission, she signed us up for the Oklahoma Senior Games in ballroom dancing about fourteen dance events. We committed to learning seven dances: waltz, tango, swing, salsa, and others. We had two different instructors: one for Smooth and one for Rhythm. For about two months, we practiced two to three times a week.

On the day of the competition, on that field and in that ballroom, we were the only African American couple. We couldn't help but stand out. But what stood out more than our skin color was our commitment to each other and to giving a great performance.

By God's grace, we received gold medals and placed first in all fourteen events. People saw the medals. What they did not see were the hard practices, the sore feet, the arguments, the corrections, and the quiet decision to remain teachable.

I was the lead in our partnership, which meant I had a lot to remember:

- The choreography for seven different dances.

- The timing and musicality.
- The frame and posture.
- The responsibility of guiding my partner across the floor with confidence and care.

I got pushed. I got corrected. I got frustrated. But I stayed teachable.

I listened to our instructors. I listened to my wife. I learned to respond to her slightest movement, to protect her on the dance floor, and to adjust when I made a mistake. I had to lay my pride down and accept that, even as a dean, I was an amateur in this space. I was not running the show; I was being trained.

That experience reminded me of something vital:

A title does not cancel the need to learn.

Elevation does not eliminate the need for correction.

Promotion does not mean graduation from God's classroom.

Lifetime learning is not just a slogan for accreditation reports; it is a survival skill for a thriving dean. God wants us to thrive, not simply in our careers, but in our marriages, our health, and our walk with Him. To thrive, we must remain coachable.

Ballroom dancing became a parable of my leadership:

- In my marriage, I am still a student.
- In my health, I am still a student.
- In my deanship, I am still a student.

When I allow God, my wife, my doctors, my colleagues, and even my critics to teach me, I become wiser, softer, and stronger. The pressure doesn't disappear, but I'm no longer facing it as a rigid, brittle leader. I'm learning to move with it, almost like a dance.

Application for Academic Leaders

Teachability is not a pleasant extra for deans; it is a vital safeguard against burnout and breakdown.

- *Teachability in health means you listen when your body speaks, when your doctor cautions you, and when your spouse says, "Something has to change."*
- *Teachability in relationships means you allow loved ones and trusted friends to tell you the truth, even when it wounds your pride.*

- *Teachability in leadership means resisting the temptation to act as though you are the most intelligent person in the room, and instead modeling what it looks like to learn, adjust, and grow.*

In a world where leaders are expected to have all the answers, you can offer your campus a powerful witness: a dean who is still growing in wisdom.

Reflection Questions

1. Where in your life is God trying to teach you something right now through stress, feedback, or a loved one's concern?
2. How has your title or experience ever made you less open to coaching, correction, or new practices?
3. What "dance floor" (marriage, health, leadership, spiritual life) is God inviting you to re-enter with a teachable spirit?

Leadership Prompt

Identify one area wherein thou hast been resisting correction: thy health habits, thy schedule, thy leadership style, or thy relationships. This week, choose one "instructor" , a spouse, mentor, physician, counselor, or trusted colleague, and intentionally seek their feedback.

Hearken without defending thyself. Take notes. Pray over that which thou hearest. Then, even as a student upon the dance floor, choose one concrete adjustment to make, for a wise leader "will increase in learning" (Proverbs 1:5).

CHAPTER 9 – VISION

Theme: Seeing Beyond the Cliff

Scripture – Proverbs 29:18
"Where there is no vision, the people perish."

Dean's Reflection

I still remember the day I walked into Dr. Sherri Smith-Keys's office, feeling the quiet, focused energy she always carries.

"Daryl," she said, "there's a radio station in Tulsa that wants me to create a show."

Most people would have heard that and thought, nice opportunity, another line on the résumé.

But I heard something different. I heard a door.

At that time, Langston University's School of Business was teetering on what folks called the "enrollment cliff." Resources were thin. Our students were mostly first-generation, many battling financial and personal storms just to stay enrolled. In some circles, people had already written us off. A few even wondered if the business school would ever truly rebound.

Yet in prayer, I kept hearing the same phrase: Tell the story.

We were doing good work, quiet miracles, really. Faculty going the extra mile. Students winning competitions. Small victories stacking up in classrooms, internships, and exam scores. But outside our walls, no one knew. Even on campus, the narrative was still trapped in yesterday's struggles.

So, when Dr. Smith-Keys mentioned that radio show, I didn't just see airtime. I saw a pulpit in the public square. I saw a platform where God could shine a light on what He was doing at Langston.

"Sherri," I said, "what if this isn't just your show? What if this is our show, Langston's voice? What if we use it to tell the stories nobody's hearing?"

She smiled. That's when I knew I had an ally in the vision.

We started dreaming out loud.

What if we created a show that wasn't stiff or academic, but soulful and real?

What if students, alumni, and community leaders could come on and share what Langston meant to them?

What if we could highlight both the challenges and the triumphs, without pretending, without sugarcoating, but with hope?

The name came next: Langston Vibes.

Not "Langston Report." Not "Business Hour." Vibes, because we wanted people to feel something when they listened: pride, possibility, joy, and perhaps a touch of conviction to do more, give more, believe more.

Of course, once the vision was born, reality sought to choke it.

Some wondered why a dean, already carrying a heavy load, would spend time on a radio show. A few quietly questioned our priorities. Were we chasing publicity instead of doing "serious" work?

But here is what they did not see: the show was the work.

Vision rarely looks efficient at first glance. It looks risky. It looks extra. It looks like something you undertake when you do not yet understand how stretched the budget and schedule already are.

Yet Proverbs 29:18 kept echoing in my spirit: "Where there is no vision, the people perish."

If we did not tell our own story, someone else would continue telling the wrong one.

So, we moved forward.

Friday afternoons, when many were winding down, we were winding up mic checks, run-downs, last-minute guest confirmations. Some days we were weary. Some days the week had been long and heavy. But once that "On Air" light came on, fatigue had to take a back seat.

We interviewed students who had overcome incredible odds to be at Langston.

We highlighted faculty who were innovating in the classroom.

We brought in community partners, pastors, and business leaders who believed in our students' futures.

Slowly, something began to shift.

What they were truly saying was, "We feel seen."

Internally, Langston Vibes became more than just a radio show. It was a mirror and a megaphone, a mirror to remind us who we truly are: resilient, creative, called; and a megaphone to ensure the world could not ignore what God was building on a small HBCU campus in Oklahoma.

Externally, it became a bridge.

We were not merely asking people to give; we were inviting them into a living, breathing story, one episode at a time. By the time we spoke seriously about scholarships, internships, and capital campaigns, many listeners already felt as though they were part of the family.

That is what vision does. It connects dots people did not know were related. It unites a dean in a suit, a nurse-executive in Tulsa, a first-generation student from down the road, and a donor across the country into the same narrative of hope.

Looking back, I see that Langston Vibes was never solely about the media. It was about ministry, the ministry of testimony.

Every episode whispered a quiet truth: God is not done with this place.

In leadership, vision is not merely the grand strategic plan on paper. It is the holy habit of looking upon a struggling situation and asking, "Lord, what could this be if Thou wouldst breathe upon it?" It is the courage to act on that answer, even when the budget says no, the calendar says impossible, and a few voices say it is unnecessary.

As a dean, I have learned that vision is tested not at the moment of inspiration but in the grind of implementation when you are driving to the station after a long week, when a guest cancels at the last minute, when numbers have not yet matched the faith, you are walking in.

Yet God confirms that which He begins. Over time, we saw the same school that some had counted out rise in national rankings, excel on standardized exams, and capture attention far beyond its size. Did the radio show cause all that? No. But it helped us see it, name it, and share it. It kept us believing that the cliff before us was not the end, it was the ledge from which God was teaching us to build wings.

Application for Academic Leaders

1. Name the story God is writing.

   Set aside 30–60 minutes to write a one-page "vision story" for your school or unit: Where are you now? Where could you be in 3–5 years if God breathed on your efforts? Share this story with your key allies (associate deans, department chairs, a trusted pastor or mentor).

2. Identify your "radio show."

   List two or three existing platforms you might be underusing: podcasts, radio, chapel moments, town halls, social media, newsletters, and alumni events. Choose one and commit to telling consistent stories of student, faculty, and community impact over the next 90 days.

3. Build with allies, not solo.

   Ask, "Who is my Dr. Sherri Smith-Keys?" Identify at least one partner inside the institution and one outside (church, community, or industry) who shares your heart. Invite them into the vision and give them real ownership of one piece of it

4. Align visibility with mission, not ego.

   Before each public initiative, pray: "Lord, let this platform glorify You and bless students, not promote my name." Use that lens to decide which invitations to accept, what stories to tell, and how to measure "success."

5. Track small confirmations.

Keep a simple "Vision Journal" where you record notes: a student's testimony, an alumni response, a new donor inquiry, improved morale, or enrollment. Revisit these entries when resistance or fatigue tempts you to pull back.

Leadership Prompt

Where is God inviting me to see beyond the cliff?

This week, choose one concrete step to advance a God- honoring vision for your school, launching a small platform, sharing a new story, or inviting a key ally into the work. Write it down, put a date beside it, and pray daily:

"Lord, sharpen my vision. Let me see this campus as You see it, and give me courage to act on what I see."

CHAPTER 10 – INNOVATION

Theme: Turning the Mundane into the Magnificent

Scripture – Proverbs 10:14
"Wise men lay up knowledge: but the mouth of the foolish is their destruction."

Theme

Innovation is not merely the act of invention; it is the transformation of ordinary systems, stale routines, and stagnant traditions into dynamic, purpose-driven experiences. Academic deans who embrace innovation challenge the status quo to enhance student learning, faculty engagement, and institutional outcomes.

Dean's Reflection

When I walked into the MG 4703 – Strategy & Policy course during my first semester as dean, I saw potential, but also challenges. The students were disengaged. The format was outdated. The results were not where they needed to be.

With Dr. Charles Mambula as my co-pilot, we reimagined the course. We did not merely tweak the syllabus; we transformed the entire experience. We embedded business simulations. We empowered student teams to lead class discussions. We hosted career readiness bootcamps. I personally attended over eighty percent of the classes, even as a sitting dean. Together, we built a culture of ownership, responsibility, and excellence.

And then came the result:

Our students scored in the top one percent nationwide on the Peregrine Business Exam, surpassing over eighty-three thousand peers across the country.

Truly, innovation, when rooted in faith and vision, becometh transformation.

Application for Academic Leaders

- What program, course, or process in your school needs an innovation overhaul?
- Innovation doesn't always mean starting from scratch. What could you restructure, reignite, or reframe to improve outcomes?
- Who are your innovation allies (i.e., faculty, students, staff) who are willing to co-create with you?

Leadership Prompt

Take 15 minutes today to reflect on an area in your school that has become "routine." Ask yourself: What would this look like if I were designing it from scratch today?

Then, schedule a 30-minute "innovation jam session" with a trusted colleague to brainstorm upgrades. Innovation loves collaboration.

CHAPTER 11 – GRACIOUS SPEECH

Theme: Honeycomb Words in Hard Times

> *Scripture – Proverbs 16:24*
> "Pleasant words are as a honeycomb, sweet to the soul, and health to the bones."

Dean's Reflection

There were times when I sat at the head of our business school meetings, watching my key subordinates act more like adversaries than colleagues. They would interrupt others, talk over them, and even publicly critique fellow faculty. Their harsh and unfiltered words discouraged the rest of the team. And in moments when they directed their hostility toward me or toward others, I felt the urge to meet fire with fire.

But I didn't. I held the line, not by silencing them with force, but by redirecting the conversation with composure and calm. Others noticed. One staff member later pulled me aside and said, "Dean, I don't know how you kept your cool, but you did."

Galatians 5 speaks of the fruit of the Spirit, and gracious speech is grounded in gentleness and self-control. Proverbs remind us that "Pleasant words are as a honeycomb, sweet to the soul, and health to the bones" (Proverbs 16:24). I leaned into that truth, choosing to let my words build bridges rather than burn them.

Application for Academic Leaders

Gracious speech in leadership isn't a weakness; it is strategic power. As deans, our words carry weight. When tensions rise, choose your tone, your timing, and the truth. Let your words de-escalate. Let them instruct. Let them lead.

Leadership Prompt

This week, identify a recurring tough conversation in your work. How can you prepare in advance to respond with graciousness? What "pleasant words" might change the dynamic in your next meeting?

CHAPTER 12 – FAITHFULNESS

Theme: Showing Up, Semester After Semester

> *Scripture – Proverbs 3:5-6*
> "Trust in the Lord with all thine heart; and lean not unto thine own understanding. In all thy ways acknowledge him, and he shall direct thy paths."

Dean's Reflection

This past season tested my faith more than any moment in my academic leadership journey. I found myself navigating difficult personnel matters, emotionally draining days, and seasons of spiritual fatigue. In moments like these, the temptation is to respond with frustration, withdraw, or depend on our own wisdom. But Proverbs reminds us that we are not to lean on our own understanding, but on God's.

There were situations where instructions were ignored, systems were bypassed, and accountability seemed like a one- way street. Despite repeated coaching and grace, I watched familiar patterns of resistance appear again. In those moments, I realized that no policy, procedure, or meeting could change what only God can shape in a person's heart.

As a leader, you sometimes feel like the one standing alone on principle. But I have learned that faith does not guarantee ease, it guarantees direction. God never left me without guidance. While away from the office, I left clear expectations, praying for a spirit of order and teamwork. What I returned to was confirmation that unresolved patterns must be addressed not with fear, but with faith.

I leaned on Galatians 6:9, which says, *"And let us not be weary in well doing: for in due season, we shall reap, if we faint not." This strengthened me to keep standing on integrity.*

Faith is not passive; it is active trust. Faith allows me to release the urge to control every outcome and instead plant seeds of righteousness in difficult soil. The results may not appear overnight, but God promises a harvest in His timing.

Application for Academic Leaders

Faithfulness in academic leadership is not glamorous; it is grounded, persistent obedience in the face of discouragement, inconsistency, and unseen labor. It is the discipline of showing up, emotionally, spiritually, and professionally, long after the excitement of the assignment has faded.

As a dean, faithfulness looks like:

- Returning to the mission daily, even when others are distracted or disengaged.

- Trusting God's timing when change feels slow or opposition feels loud.

- Leading with consistency. Faithfulness means you don't change your standards, tone, or expectations based on who is watching. Your campus should know what to expect from your leadership—clarity, integrity, and fairness.

- Anchoring decisions in scripture, not emotion. When frustration rises or support feels thin, return to Proverbs 3:5 -6. Let God straighten the paths you cannot untangle.

Faithfulness is doing what is right before God, even when the results are delayed, uncelebrated, or misunderstood.

Leadership Prompt

When have you faced a professional situation where doing the right thing felt isolating? How did your faith anchor you? Write down a moment when endurance, not emotion, carried you through.

CHAPTER 13 – SELF-CONTROL

Theme: Discipline Before Emotion

Scripture – Proverbs 25:28
"He that has no rule over his own spirit is like a city that is broken down, and without walls."

Dean's Reflection

It's easy to lead when everything is running smoothly. But what happens when an employee, despite being corrected multiple times, continues to disregard processes, ignore tasks, and undermine authority? I experienced this firsthand. Despite several reminders, this employee still failed to meet university expectations. This behavior confused other staff members, who began to see these actions as acceptable. As a dean, I couldn't ignore the example being set. Yet even with a valid cause for concern, I had to watch how I responded.

Self-control required documenting every interaction. It required holding back the urge to react emotionally. HR processes are slow, and in a culture that values loyalty over performance, it was tempting to give up. But leadership demands persistence and emotional discipline. I remembered what Proverbs says: "He that has no rule over his own spirit is like a city that is broken down, and without walls" (Proverbs 25:28, KJV). Instead of letting my emotions lead, I chose to stay guarded, deliberate, and professional.

Application for Academic Leaders

True leadership is proven in times of crisis. Self-control keeps our leadership fortress strong, whether you are issuing a reprimand or facing resistance. Lead with integrity, not impulse.

Leadership Prompt

Where in your leadership are you tempted to lose control through anger, frustration, or avoidance? What would "city walls" look like in that area? Take one step this week to strengthen them.

CHAPTER 14 – COURAGE

Theme: Standing Firm in the Spotlight

Scripture – Proverbs 3:25–26
"Be not afraid of sudden fear, neither of the desolation of the wicked, when it cometh.
For the LORD shall be thy confidence, and shall keep thy foot from being taken."

Dean's Reflection

When I arrived as dean in 2024, I had a straightforward plan: listen first, change later.

My intention was to spend the first year observing how things worked, building trust, and learning the culture. No sudden moves. No major shifts. After all, what wise leader steps into a new organization and starts restructuring in the very first year?

But once I began listening to students, faculty, staff, and even the data, the truth refused to stay quiet.

Students were complaining. Some concerns were minor, but many were serious: advising gaps, inconsistent classroom experiences, confusion about requirements, and a steady stream of stories all pointing in the same direction, we were losing students we should have been graduating. Our graduation and retention rates confirmed that reality.

Meanwhile, some key leaders in the organization tried to reassure me that everything was fine.

"Students lie."

"We just got through accreditation without you."

"Things are okay. Don't rock the boat."

On paper, the school had "passed." In reality, the house was cracking.

I found myself standing between two narratives:

- One from students, data, and my own observations saying, "We are in trouble."
- Another from leadership voices saying, "We're good. Don't make waves."

That tension put me in a very uncomfortable spot. The administration questioned my decision to restructure leadership. Some wondered why I was pushing for change so quickly. Why reorganize departments? Why shift reporting lines? Why disturb what had "worked" well enough to survive the last review?

But the more I prayed, the clearer it became: we could not move forward with the same thinking that had brought us here. Decades of leadership turnover and faculty decline told a sobering story; if we did nothing, the school would continue to drift, and our students would ultimately pay the price.

So, with fear in my stomach but faith in my heart, I moved forward with the restructuring. It was not impulsive; it was prayed over, documented, and rooted in a clear vision for student success and long-term stability.

There was a cost. In the short run, I lost faculty.

Some people chose to leave rather than adapt to the new structure. Some relationships shifted. Some doors closed.

But something else happened too:

- The faculty and staff who remained became more focused.
- The chemistry improved.
- The mission became clearer.
- We began building a culture where doing right by students mattered more than keeping broken systems comfortable.

Courage is not the absence of fear; it is the choice to obey God even in the midst of opposition, confusion, and risk.

Some deans avoid confrontation at all costs, and I understand why. Confrontation can threaten your job, your reputation, and even your relationships. And to be fair, not every conflict is a simple matter of "good versus evil." Sometimes the lines are blurred, the history is complicated, and well-meaning people sincerely disagree.

But there are moments when the fog lifts just enough for you to see that silence would be a form of complicity. In such moments, God does not call us to be reckless; He calls us to be bold as a lion (cf. Proverbs 28:1, KJV).

In my story at Langston, courage looked like:

- Trusting what students told me, even when it was inconvenient.
- Trusting the data, even when it challenged the comfortable narrative that "everything is fine."
- Trusting God enough to step out of my comfort for the sake of long-term health.

In the end, I had to choose whose voice would define reality:

- The voice that said, "Don't rock the boat,"

  or

- The still, small voice saying, "You were not sent here to uphold a broken system."

I chose to trust God. And He met me in the restructuring, not with instant applause, but with quiet confirmation, clearer vision, and a faculty core that shared a renewed sense of purpose.

Courage matters.

Application for Academic Leaders

Courage in academic leadership is not about being loud; it is about being faithful when:

- The evidence points one way while the politics pull you another.
- You know in your spirit that "business as usual" is harming students.
- You are tempted to protect your position rather than protect your mission.

For deans and academic leaders, courage may look like:

- Naming uncomfortable truths about retention, graduation, or institutional climate.
- Restructuring roles or programs that no longer serve students well.
- Pushing back respectfully but firmly, against narratives that minimize real problems

In closing, the goal is not to "win" against colleagues, but to stand for God's truth on behalf of your students and the future of your institution. As scripture reminds us, "Be strong and of a good courage;

be not afraid, neither be thou dismayed: for the LORD thy God is with thee whithersoever thou goest." (Joshua 1:9)

Reflection Questions

1. Where are you sensing a gap between "the official story" and what students, data, or your own spirit are telling you?
2. What decision have you been postponing out of fear of conflict, criticism, or loss?
3. How might remembering Proverbs 28:1 ("...the righteous are bold as a lion") reshape your next leadership move?

Leadership Prompt

Identify one specific area in your school where you know change is needed but fear or politics have held you back.

This week:

- Write down the reality as you see it. Facts, student voices, and data.
- Bring it before God in prayer and ask for *lion-hearted courage* and wise strategy.
- Take one concrete step of courage, start the hard conversation, draft the restructuring proposal, or clearly name the issue in a leadership meeting.

Trust that the same God who called you to this role will give you the courage to lead, not just occupy the seat.

CHAPTER 15 – PRUDENCE

Theme: Thinking Before "Reply All"

> *Scripture – Proverbs 14:8*
> "The wisdom of the prudent is to understand his way."

Dean's Reflection

Prudence is what you practice when you would rather react.

As dean, I have faced more personnel issues than I ever expected, reprimands, repeated non-compliance, and, in rare cases, terminations. Some employees were openly insubordinate: arguing with directives, challenging decisions in front of others, or disregarding clear instructions altogether.

In those moments, my emotions wanted to take the lead: frustration, disappointment, even anger. But prudence reminded me of this simple truth: emotion cannot be your strategy.

So instead, I chose a different path:

- I carefully documented every instance where employees were diverting from established requirements and policies.
- I held numerous formal and informal meetings, giving each person the opportunity to respond and correct their course.
- I partnered with HR, even when the process felt slow and cumbersome.
- I remained calm in conversations where others became heated.

Some deans avoid direct conflict, hoping that problems will "work themselves out." I have learned the opposite: avoiding accountability only creates bigger, more painful problems in the long run, for the team, for the students, and even for the person in trouble.

In some cases, employees responded positively to coaching and accountability. Their performance improved, and relationships were restored. Sadly, in other cases, they did not. Hard decisions had to be made.

Prudence did not remove the pain of those decisions, but it ensured that when I acted, I had:

- Thoughtfully considered the consequences.
- Followed the proper processes.
- Gave people fair warning and opportunity.
- Acted from conviction, not impulse.

That is the wisdom of the prudent: to give thought to their ways.

Application for Academic Leaders

- Prudence is disciplined foresight.

- Slow thy reactions. Before sending the email, making the decision, or confronting the issue, pause and consider: “What shall this set in motion?”
- Document diligently. When it comes to personnel matters, your memory is not enough. Clear, detailed notes will protect you, your institution, and even the employee.
- Follow policy and seek counsel. Walk in step with HR or legal guidance; go not alone in crafting thine own system.
- Distinguish between pattern and incident. Prudence giveth thee sight to discern whether a behavior is but a one-time mistake or a long-term pattern demanding intervention.

Leadership Prompt

Identify one personnel or structural issue you’ve been avoiding because it feels messy. Set aside time this week to:

1. Review the facts and documentation.
2. Pray for wisdom and self-control.
3. Take one prudent step forward, an honest conversation, a clarified expectation, or a documented warning.

CHAPTER 16 – GENEROSITY

Theme: Open Hands, Full Heart

Scripture – Proverbs 11:25
"The liberal soul shall be made fat: and he that watereth shall be watered also."

Dean's Reflection

Many of our students at Langston are first-generation college students, navigating higher education with courage and very limited financial safety nets. Their families are proud, but often stretched to the breaking point.

One semester, I reviewed the data and discovered that more than 200 business students owed the university over one million dollars combined. If a student owed more than about two hundred dollars in the spring, they could not enroll in the next semester or graduate. A few hundred dollars stood between them and their future.

I was moved to action.

Almost every semester, our business school began providing financial retention scholarships so that students could clear small balances and move forward, either registering for classes or walking across the graduation stage. This was not because we suddenly found extra money in the budget, but because generous corporate partners and individual donors responded to the need.

We watched God multiply gifts from corporations, local businesses, alumni, and friends into life-changing interventions for our students.

I will never forget the look on a student's face when I told them, "We found a way. You can graduate." They didn't see the spreadsheets, pledge forms, or phone calls. They just saw God's provision.

Generosity, I've learned, is not a line item, it is a posture:

- Open hands with money.
- Open doors with opportunities.
- Open hearts with time and attention.

As deans, we may either hoard our influence or use it to refresh others. Every time I choose generosity, I see Proverbs 11:25 come to life: "The liberal soul shall be made fat: and he that watereth shall be watered also." As we refresh others, God refreshes us.

Application for Academic Leaders

Generosity is a strategic ministry.

- Name the need clearly. Donors and partners respond when you articulate specific gaps (for example, "balances under $1,000 that prevent graduation").
- Tie generosity to outcomes. Show how even small gifts help real students stay enrolled and progress toward their degrees.
- Model personal giving. Modest personal contributions signal your belief in the mission you are asking others to support.
- Celebrate every blessing. Publicly and privately thank donors, partners, and staff who make generosity possible.

Leadership Prompt

What is one specific, practical way you could practice generosity this month as a dean, not just as an individual (e.g., a micro-scholarship, a travel opportunity, a book fund, or an honorarium for adjuncts)?

Write it down, pray over it, and ask God to send the right partners.

CHAPTER 17 – FEAR OF THE LORD

Theme: Leading for an Audience of One

Scripture – Proverbs 1:7
"The fear of the Lord is the beginning of knowledge."

Dean's Reflection

One of the great joys of my deanship has been taking students off campus to behold what is possible. In November, we were blessed to take fifteen students and a total of twenty souls to the Dallas Cowboys Career Panel at AT&T Stadium.

We were not merely going to see a football field; we were going to witness, up close, the workings of sports, media, and leadership.

On this trip, something holy happens before the bus ever moves. One of our business professors gathers us for prayer. I am not foolish. Deans carry a heavy burden. Students depend on us. Who do deans depend upon?

Deans need God too! We give thanks unto God for safety, for favor, for opportunity. We beseech Him to open doors, to open minds, and to open eyes. We entreat Him to cover us on the road, and to protect students from dangers both seen and unseen.

The same spiritual needs occur on campus. Sometimes, students come to me with grievous burdens: deaths in the family, mental afflictions, broken relationships, or financial emergencies. When it is met, and when they are willing, I ask, "Wouldst thou mind if I pray for you?"

Oftentimes, they consent, with tears in their eyes. In those moments, I am not a dean; I am a brother in faith, standing in the gap.

This trait is what the fear of the Lord looks like in my leadership:

- I recognize that I ultimately answer to God, and not merely to presidents, provosts, or accreditors.
- I regard students, faculty, and staff as souls, and not only as roles.
- I invite God's presence into buses, offices, meetings, and events, not for display, but as a necessity.

The fear of the Lord is not terror; it is reverent awareness. It is guiding each day before an Audience of One.

Application for Academic Leaders

The fear of the Lord shall guide thy decisions according to the heart of God.

- Begin key meetings and journeys with prayer, where it is met and permitted, seeking the wisdom and protection of the Almighty.

- Remember whose Name thou dost ultimately bear; let that knowledge govern thy handling of power, riches, and men.
- Be spiritually present, not only administratively. When students or colleagues bring thee into their affliction, weigh whether prayer is meet and welcome.
- Let the scriptures direct thy policies. Though thou must obey the rules of thy institution, let the Word of God determine thy tone, justice, and mercy.

Leadership Prompt

Reflect on one recent decision or event. If you had led it with a heightened awareness of the fear of the Lord, what might you have done differently, if anything?

Ask God to deepen your reverence in one specific area of your leadership this week.

CHAPTER 18 – TRUSTWORTHINESS

Theme: A Safe Place for Hard Truths

> *Scripture – Proverbs 11:13*
> "A talebearer revealeth secrets: but he that is of a faithful spirit concealeth the matter."

Dean's Reflection

Trust is a form of currency in academic leadership. People do not invest significant resources in leaders they do not trust.

We were planning to take students to a career event with the Oklahoma City Thunder, the 2025 NBA Champions. We needed to charter a bus, which is a considerable expense for an underfunded HBCU business school.

Around that time, my colleague and friend, Dr. Robert Shepard, visited our campus. He spoke with our students in class and witnessed firsthand the hunger, potential, and humility they carried.

Afterward, he pulled me aside.

He and his wife felt led to donate the full amount needed for the charter bus.

He trusted me.

He trusted our team.

He trusted that if he invested in us, the money would go exactly where we said it would go to provide students with a life-shaping experience.

His gift was not random. We had worked together before. He had observed my leadership in other settings. That history of integrity and follow-through became the fertile soil in which generosity could grow.

The same is true for our corporate partners. They entrust us with scholarship funds, travel stipends, and program support because they believe we will:

- Tell the truth concerning needs and outcomes.
- Steward resources with diligence.
- Keep our word.

Trustworthiness is established by faithful decisions, one at a time, yet it may be swiftly lost when confidential stories or funds are mishandled.

As a dean, I aspire to be the kind of leader in whom students, colleagues, donors, and presidents may confide, assured that their stories and investments shall be handled with care.

Application for Academic Leaders

Trustworthiness is a form of stewardship. As you consider what others share with you, ask yourself:

- Guard confidences. When students or colleagues share sensitive information, resist turning it into a story. Protect their dignity.
- Be precise and honest about money. Report clearly how funds are used and build simple, transparent systems.
- Do what you say you will do. If you promise to follow up, follow up. If circumstances change, communicate quickly and humbly.
- Remember: trust is slow to build and quick to break. Treat it as sacred.

Leadership Prompt

Think of one relationship with a donor, colleague, or student, where trust is high. What behaviors helped build that trust?

Now think of an area where trust may be fragile. What one step can you take this week to strengthen it?

CHAPTER 19 – JOY

Theme: Smiling in the Storm

> *Scripture – Proverbs 13:12*
> "Hope deferred maketh the heart sick: but when the desire cometh, it is a tree of life."

Dean's Reflection

I attended my first Langston University graduation as dean in May 2024. By that time, I had come to know several seniors personally. They would stop by my office, sit upon the couch, and speak of life, family pressures, financial struggles, and doubts about finishing.

Some of them had been on the brink of dropping out. Small balances had almost hindered others. A few had quietly wondered if any in leadership truly cared whether they would reach the end.

On graduation day, I was not merely seated upon the platform. I was in line with them, marching forth toward the football field where the ceremony was held.

I listened to the roar of parents and friends as each group emerged, shouts, cowbells, tears, and laughter. Behind every name the announcer read was a story I did not fully know, but the Lord did. (Psalm 139:2–3)

As we moved forward, I beheld some of "my" students in that line, students who had sat in my office, who had written to me in times of crisis, who had benefited from retention scholarships or from the extra patience of faculty. Now they were robed in cap and gown, moments away from crossing the stage.

That was joy.

Not the shallow joy of all things being easy, but the deep joy of witnessing God's faithfulness made manifest in tassels and diplomas.

Joy, for me as a dean, is:

- Hearing a student say, "I thought I should not make it, but I have prevailed."
- Observing families rejoice over a first-generation graduate.
- Knowing that behind the scenes, through meetings, emails, prayers, and policies, God employed our imperfect labors to bring them to this day.

In a role fraught with conflict and crisis, one must purposefully seek and cherish these moments. Joy is not a luxury; it is a balm unto the soul.

Application for Academic Leaders

Joy sustains you through the grind.

- Attend graduation with thine heart open, not merely thy regalia upon thee. Look for the faces and stories that remind thee why thou dost this work.
- Celebrate small victories, not only the great rankings and at-risk students restored, but also a faculty innovation, a mended relationship.
- Share stories of joy in meetings and in thy writings, that thy team may remember the impact behind the labor.

- Guard thy time for gratitude. Give thanks unto God continually for students, colleagues, and opportunities.

Leadership Prompt

Write down the name of one student whose success has brought you joy. Take a moment to thank God for them and, if appropriate, send them a short note of congratulations or encouragement.

CHAPTER 20 – COLLABORATION

Theme: Sharpened by Others

> *Scripture – Proverbs 27:17*
> "Iron sharpeneth iron; so, a man sharpeneth the countenance of his friend."

Dean's Reflection

In 2025, we hosted the Howard University x PNC Entrepreneur Summit at Langston University. It was historic, a first-of-its-kind event that brought together our students, faculty, corporate partners, and the Town of Langston.

We did not merely hold a panel and call it a day. We conducted a student pitch competition with real prize money. We invited community leaders, pastors, local business owners, and neighbors. More than one hundred people participated.

What moved me most was not only the content, but the chemistry in the room.

- Students from an HBCU in rural Oklahoma were learning from leaders connected to Howard University and PNC.
- Town residents, who had sometimes felt disconnected from campus, were seated at the same tables as students and corporate guests.
- Faculty were networking with practitioners, not merely reading about them.

For a moment, you could feel it: we were not isolated. We were part of a larger ecosystem of Black excellence, entrepreneurship, and innovation.

Community and collaboration are not mere buzzwords; they are survival strategies. Langston's business school cannot "dominate the state" in isolation. We need:

- Other HBCUs and PWIs, like Oklahoma State University, through our 4+1 MOU.
- Corporate partners.
- Churches and civic groups.
- Alumni and local leaders.

When we collaborate well, all are sharpened:

- Students gain broader networks and opportunities.
- Faculty discern new directions for teaching and research.
- Partners perceive the value of investing in our campus.
- The town regards the university as a neighbor, not a stranger.

Events like the HU x PNC Summit remind me of Proverbs 27:17: "Iron sharpeneth iron; so, a man sharpeneth the countenance of his friend." God never intended for us to rebuild walls alone.

Application for Academic Leaders

- Community and collaboration expand your capacity:
- Host events that intentionally mix groups of students, faculty, community, and corporate partners. Design them for interaction, not merely speeches.
- Pursue strategic MOUs, like 4+1 pathways, which grant your students access to resources your institution does not possess.
- Involve your town and alumni. Do not merely invite them to donate; invite them to participate.
- Regard collaboration as discipleship. The partners you choose shape your students' vision of what is possible.

Leadership Prompt

List two potential partners, one campus-based (another department or school) and one external (church, company, or community group). What is one step you can take this month to explore a collaborative initiative that would bless your students?

CHAPTER 21: HUMOR

Theme: Laughing Without Losing Reverence

Scripture – Proverbs 17:22
"A merry heart doeth good like a medicine: but a broken spirit drieth the bones."

Dean's Reflection

Every Wednesday, the academic deans at our university meet with the VPAA on Zoom. One week, a very professional dean was sharing her detailed thoughts when I assumed she had finished. I began speaking, only to hear her voice chime in again. She had activated the Zoom "raised hand" reaction.

"Excuse me, Dean Green," she said sharply, "I'm not finished."

Without missing a beat, I smiled and replied, "Excuse me, Dean, I saw your hand raised. I thought thou wert praising the Lord."

There was silence, then laughter. I had broken the tension.

Humor has always been one of my tools of leadership. It buildeth bridges. It healeth wounds. It disarms stress. Whether I am engaging students, faculty, or administrators, I have found that laughter inviteth connection and vulnerability.

In the academic world, pressure is a good thing. Yet a little joy can lighten a heavy room. Humor remindeth us that we are but men. As deans, we need that medicine.

Application for Leaders

- Identify one situation this week where you are tempted to withdraw or go silent. What would it look like to stay engaged with grace instead?
- Name one student, colleague, or staff member who especially needs you to live out this virtue in a tangible way. Decide what you will do and when.

- In prayer, ask God to show you any motives—fear, pride, or fatigue—that might be dulling your response to His call in this area, and invite Him to realign your heart.

Leadership Prompt

Where can you use laughter to disarm tension in your environment? Can you be both professional and joyful? Share a recent moment where humor brought clarity or comfort to your leadership.

CONCLUSION

When the Smoke Finally Shows

Years before I ever sat in a dean's chair, I drove past a campus that went from light to dark almost overnight.

St. Gregory's University was a beautiful Catholic institution in Oklahoma, a place of history, tradition, and quiet faith. One day, it was alive: students walking between buildings, lights glowing in dorm windows, banners fluttering in the Oklahoma wind. Not long after, it was an empty shell. The doors were closed. The lights were off. The campus was still.

In conversations with people connected to St. Gregory's, a pattern emerged: many students and faculty felt blindsided. They knew there were challenges, of course, but they did not see the closure coming. For them, there had been no alarm, only a notice. No time to move, only time to grieve.

That image haunts me.

Some schools burn with flames. Others burn quietly, from the inside out, under the weight of debt, denial, and delayed decisions. By the time the smoke is visible to everyone, it is often too late.

When I later arrived at Langston University's School of Business, St. Gregory's was never far from my mind. I could see the same ingredients that had brought down other institutions: structural underfunding, enrollment pressures, accreditation warnings, exhausted faculty, and a culture that had grown accustomed to living with risk.

In the end, the story of Langston University School of Business is not about me; it is about what God can do when there is much prayer, a holy urgency, and a willingness to rebuild broken walls in hostile territory.

When I arrived in the Spring of 2024, I was handed what some openly called "the worst organization on campus," a program with declining enrollment, conditional accreditation, low morale, and a reputation for complaints rather than excellence. Yet, eighteen months later, by the grace of God, that very school has become one of the university's most remarkable comeback stories. Enrollment has surged from about 270 students to more than 400, a more than fifty percent increase, which has generated millions in new revenue for the institution and renewed hope for our community. Our seniors now rank among the top 1% nationally on the Peregrine Business Exam, competing against over 83,000 students across 13 business disciplines. We have been recognized as a top Thirty HBCU business school, and external partners who once overlooked Langston now seek us out.

In less than two years, the Lord allowed us to accomplish more than I ever imagined when I first walked into that burning- building culture. The list is not exhaustive, but it is enough to show that God truly met us at Langston and moved quickly. A summary of several key milestones appears in Table 1: Selected Legacy Accomplishments as Dean of the Langston University School of Business (2024–2026).

At Oklahoma Baptist University, long before Langston, the Lord began teaching me the importance of personal philanthropy. My mentors made it clear: leaders do not just ask others to give; they give themselves. That conviction followed me to Langston, an HBCU where the majority of our business students carry significant financial need and many are first- generation college students. In one semester alone, more than 200 business majors owed the university over $1 million collectively; for many, a past-due balance of just $200–$1,000 stood between them and re-enrolling or graduating. By God's grace, and through the generosity of corporate partners and individual donors, we have been able to award $20,000–$30,000 in strategic retention scholarships each term to close those gaps. Flowing from that same conviction, the majority of the proceeds from this book will be directed to student scholarships and faculty development. Working with my publisher, we are establishing an endowed fund at Langston University as part of my legacy—because for me, generosity is not simply a topic to write about; it is a way to live and to finish well.

Table 1. Selected Legacy Accomplishments as Dean of the Langston University School of Business (2024–2026)

	Area	Accomplishments
1	National Learning Outcomes	In Fall 2025, graduating business seniors scored in the top 1% nationally on the Peregrine Business Exam (13 critical subject areas like accounting, finance) for the second time, under fully proctored, in-class conditions, demonstrating true mastery rather than test prep alone.
2	Dean-Led Scholarships	Launched the Dean D. Green Endowed Fund for Hope & Innovation and a companion dean-led business scholarship—the first scholarships ever initiated by a business school dean at Langston. These funds are designed to support student retention and reward leadership and academic excellence, with an initial goal of raising $20,000 to seed and sustain this work.

	Area	Accomplishments
3	Concurrent Enrollment Breakthrough	Implemented a concurrent enrollment section of FN 2123 – Personal Finance for approximately 40 students from Millwood High School, taught by Professor Ken Daughty. This created one of the highest recent enrollments of non-degree-seeking students in university history and opened a new pipeline into business education.
4	Historic Curriculum & Micro-credentials	Led a major 2025 overhaul of the business curriculum that created a record 15 stackable micro-credentials (including leadership, personal finance, and entrepreneurship), positioning Langston as an innovator in flexible, workforce-relevant education.
5	Entrepreneurial Organizational Model	Restructured the business school to operate as an entrepreneurial, flat organization in response to faculty shortages, recruiting 28 distinguished adjuncts and achieving a record 7 on-ground instructors in a semester so students could regain a true residential learning experience. When Dr. Green arrived in 2024, the majority of business courses were online. Students were frustrated.

	Area	Accomplishments
6	Second Chance Pell Turnaround	Revamped the Second Chance Pell Program at Dick Conner Correctional Center. When Dr. Green arrived, the program was in jeopardy of shutting down. Working with Professor Mustaf Gobaba, the team stabilized the business degree pathway inside the prison; Langston is now on track to graduate 8 incarcerated students with business degrees—a first in university history.
7	IBM SkillsBuild Integration	Initiated the use of IBM SkillsBuild so that every business student has the opportunity to earn professional certificates in AI and Data Analytics at no cost, enhancing their competitiveness in an evolving job market.
8	Improved Climate & Quality of Life	Used annual faculty and student satisfaction surveys (2024–2025) and a data-driven approach to implement changes in communication, advising, and classroom engagement, resulting in measurable improvements in perceptions of support, morale, and overall quality of the academic experience.

	Area	Accomplishments
9	Targeted Retention Scholarships	Coordinated $15,000–$30,000 each semester in targeted retention scholarships, funded by corporate partners and individual donors, to help students clear modest account balances and stay enrolled or graduate on time.
10	High-Impact Faculty Development	Secured all-expense-paid participation for four faculty members—Dr. Hamilton, Dr. Mambula, Dr. Chowdhury, and Dr. White—in the Harvard University Case Method Workshop (summer 2024 and 2025), bringing world-class pedagogy back to Langston classrooms.
11	Regional Economic Engagement	Partnered with the Town of Langston and the Logan County Economic Development Council on multiple initiatives, including internships and consulting projects, to infuse fresh ideas and innovation into local government and business while giving students meaningful, community-embedded experience.

	Area	Accomplishments
12	Student Engagement & Belonging	Established a new DECA chapter and reinstated the Delta Mu Delta Business Honor Society to create stronger pathways for leadership, recognition, and community among business majors—intentionally building a sense of belonging and supporting higher retention for Langston University students.

None of this came to pass in a vacuum. It arose in the context of opposition, resistance, and spiritual warfare, some from without the institution, and some from within. There were moments when it would have been easier to keep my head down, protect my reputation, and quietly ride out my contract. But God did not send me to Langston for comfort; He sent me to bring Light into a place grown accustomed to shadows, to confront apathy with urgency, hopelessness with vision, and fear with faith.

If I am honest, there were nights when I questioned whether I had misheard God. The battles over staffing, budgets, culture, personality, and power often seemed greater than I could bear. Yet over and over, the Spirit reminded me, "This is not about thy skill; it is about Mine glory."

Any ranking, partnership, revenue growth, or national recognition we have received is not a monument to my leadership; it is a testimony of what God can accomplish when a broken vessel is yielded to His purposes.

You may be a dean, provost, department chair, or president, standing in your own version of Langston, overwhelmed by history, constrained by resources, misunderstood by colleagues, and bearing the weight of other people's decisions. You may be striving to rebuild walls with people who are not yet sure they desire them rebuilt. You may be confronting your own version of "the worst organization on campus."

But that is as it should be.

The point was never for me to be the hero of this story. The point was for God to be glorified in a school that many had already counted out, proving that He can still breathe life into dry bones, rebuild broken walls, and light up dark offices.

So, as you close this devotional, I invite you to picture two buildings:

One, like St. Gregory's, silent and shuttered, a reminder of what happens when alarms are missed.

Another, like Langston's business school, is still standing for now with its lights on, its students moving, and its future hanging partly on what leaders like you choose to do next.

In which building are you serving today?

Do you smell smoke?

Do you see cracks in the walls?

Do you hear the faint beeping of alarms that others have learned to tune out?

If so, take heart. You are not crazy, you are called.

Lead with urgency, but not fear.

Pray with desperation, but not despair.

Give with open hands, even when resources are tight.

Tell the truth, even when it costs you.

And remember: your assignment is not to save the building by yourself. Your assignment is to be faithful in your watch to sound the alarm, to rebuild what you can, to love the people God has placed inside those walls, and to leave behind something that will bless them long after your name is off the office door.

This is my story as a dean.

Now, wherever God has stationed you at a flagship, a regional, an HBCU, a community college, or a small school few have heard of, may you pick up your brick, listen for His voice, and rebuild the wall in front of you.

While there is still time.

"Dr. Daryl D. Green's spiritually enticing holy devotional embraces the reverence for God as the foundation of wisdom! These daily reflections invite not only scholars but educational leaders to deepen your faith journey from the source of ALL WISDOM, our 'Almighty God.'"

Psalm 111:10 (KJV)

— Charles J. Mambula, PhD
Director, Entrepreneurship Studies, Langston University,
Global Trade & Small Business

"I wholeheartedly endorse Dr. Daryl Green's new devotional book on leadership. I have collaborated with him for the past two years on various projects, and I've witnessed his exceptional insights and practical strategies in action. This book is a testament to his passion for empowering others and will inspire leaders at all levels."

— Dr. Sherri Smith-Keys
Associate Vice President for Clinical Affairs and
Executive Director of Langston University-Tulsa

"Commit thy works unto the Lord, and thy thoughts shall be established." — Proverbs 16:3

As Second Chance Pell Program Coordinator, I have watched purpose-driven leadership transform more than plans. It transforms people. In the unpredictable world of correctional education, Dr. Green led with clear intent, grounding decisions in calling rather than circumstance, and that clarity became our anchor. Under his leadership, we built a structure where there was fragmentation, rigor where expectations were uneven, and belief where doubt had long lived. Our students were not treated as exceptions, but as scholars entrusted with a serious opportunity. They began to lead themselves differently, showing up with discipline, accountability, and vision. When leaders commit the work to purpose, students start to see themselves not through the lens of their past, but through the promise of who they are becoming.

— Malayna S. Hasmanis, MPA, M.Ed.
Doctoral Candidate,
Second Chance Pell Program Coordinator and Adjunct Instructor,
Langston University – Dick Conner Correctional Center

"The Dean's Devotional offers a thoughtful, faith-centered approach to leadership in higher education. Through reflective prompts woven throughout, Dr. Green encourages readers to self-examine and lead with patience, humility, and wisdom. This devotional affirms that spiritual resilience is essential to effective leadership, revealing God's presence in extraordinary insights and the steady cadence of daily responsibility, making it a timely and

meaningful contribution to leadership in academia."

—Jaquita Bruner
Trustee, Town of Langston, Oklahoma

"Who could better author such an educational essay than Dr. Green.

Dr. Green's quick wit tempered with his faith and passion for student development and leadership makes him more than capable of putting into words the practices and principles of academic leadership as a pillar of professional development for encouraging educators at all levels."

— C. L. Prevost III
Management Development Coordinator
Gordon Cooper Technology Center

"Dr. Daryl Green's leadership is profound in igniting growth in individuals and empowering leaders. He leads with wisdom, humility, and unwavering faith, creating an environment where all feel seen, supported, and challenged to rise. Rather than merely managing systems, he shepherds people—transforming uncertainty into clarity and discouragement into belief. The Dean's Devotional reflects the same wisdom, humility, and faith- driven leadership that students like me have experienced and admired firsthand."

— Kobe Law
Graduating Senior

"In The Dean's Devotional, Dr. Green reveals the unseen spiritual weight of academic leadership and how faith sustains leaders through responsibility and challenge.
As a student and Dr. Green's mentee, I found this book deeply moving and reassuring. Academic leadership carries profound responsibility, one that cannot be carried without God's guidance and sustaining presence. This book is a powerful reminder that God is present in every aspect of leadership. It speaks truth with grace."

"If God is for us, who can be against us?" — Romans 8:31

— Rachel Francis
Freshman (Student)

"For nearly thirty years, I have watched Dr. Green grow as a devoted husband, father, engineer, and faithful servant at Payne Avenue Missionary Baptist Church. From his ordination as a deacon to his leadership of the deacon ministry and his mentorship of young men in our congregation, he has consistently led with passion, integrity, and compassion. His commitment to education—culminating in his doctorate —and his dedication to uplifting others have long made him a model leader within our church and community.

In The Dean's Devotional, Dr. Green offers the same wisdom and faith-driven guidance that have shaped his life and leadership. As I navigated my own season of grief after my husband's passing, the chapter on teachability especially resonated with me, reminding me that life's dances—simple or complex—require discipline, grace, and reliance on God's wisdom. This devotional is a powerful resource for leaders in any field, illustrating how Dr. Green faced challenges with steadfast faith and a commitment to serving others. His work will undoubtedly inspire and transform all who read it."

— Minister Kirktenia W. Brown
Associate Minister/Payne Avenue Missionary Baptist Church
Knoxville, Tennessee

"Witnessing Dr. Green's tenure at Langston University, I have seen firsthand how he literally and metaphorically 'turned on the lights' for a generation of students seeking hope and direction. The Dean's Devotional is more than a leadership guide; it is a blueprint for rebuilding broken walls through the power of spiritual wisdom and unshakeable faith. Dr. Green captures the true weight of the chair, reminding us that authentic leadership requires the courage to fight for those who cannot fight for themselves. This book is a mandatory playbook for any leader dedicated to transforming their community from the inside out."

— Reese "DaProphet" Brown
Graduate Student, Campus Director, Historically Black
Since LU

"The Dean's Devotional is a timely resource for academic leaders seeking to lead with purpose and spiritual grounding. Dr. Green skillfully connects the wisdom of Proverbs with the real- world demands of higher education leadership, offering thoughtful reflection for those serving in complex roles. This devotional affirms that God is present not only in our calling, but actively involved in the everyday choices that shape our leadership. It is a meaningful guide for deans and administrators committed to

leading with excellence, integrity, and faith."

— Rev. Dr. Keith Toles Jr.
Program Director of Graduate Programs in Business,
Southern Nazarene University
Senior Pastor, St. Paul Baptist Church #1

Awakening the Talents Within is a powerful, step-by-step approach that individuals can use to solve problems and contribute to their overall success. This book is a wake-up call for the next generation of leaders. Green uses his charismatic style for today's hip-hop culture, dealing with a wide range of issues, from stopping procrastination to creating business ownership. The solutions contained in the book reflect more than ten years of managing, consulting, and teaching in government, non- profit, business, and private and academic institutions.

Book Publishing for Professionals provides the secrets to gaining this useful power. Packed with proven insights and advice, this book offers a simple, logical step-by-step process for professionals. It includes effective writing tools, the best publishing options, and marketing strategies to make your book successful in the marketplace. It is geared toward the writer who wants to write a non-fiction book (biography, cookbook, self-help, Christian book, textbook, etc.).

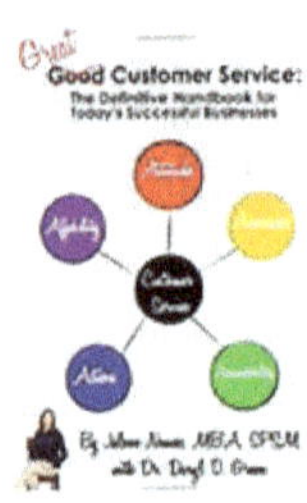

Great Customer Service: The Definitive Handbook for Today's Successful Business, co-authored with Jalene Nemec, provides a framework for businesses that want sustainable success in an unstable economy. The book appeals to salespeople and anyone who wants to maintain good relationships with their customers. Readers can ensure success by following the practical application of concepts outlined in the book in order to satisfy customers' needs or wants. The book addresses the topics of building a more profitable business, increasing good sustainable customer service, inspiring workers toward great organizational performance, and learning how to inspire demanding customers.

Breaking Organizational Ties provides practical strategies for employees attempting to cope with jobs or environments which they hate. While most managers are only concerned with the bottom line, they leave their employees vulnerable to the casualties of competitive markets. This book will enable readers to (a) learn how to survive and even enjoy their time at work even in a hostile environment, (b) gain greater confidence in their ability to grow while in a downsizing organization, and (c) discover the insight to go beyond your limitations by breaking the barriers of your self-doubt.

Don't be an Old Fool: Common Sense & Gratitude is a collection of Dr. Green's syndicated columns throughout the years. The book offers practical strategies for individuals who desire to make better decisions in their lives by using sound, common-sense approaches. With a new sense of direction, individuals will be able to re-energize themselves for the future.

Impending Danger: The Federal Handbook for Rethinking Leadership in the 21st century provides critical answers regarding how government leaders can reduce partisan bickering by changing the current leadership paradigm. With forty years' worth of experience in the public sector, Dr. Green and his co-author, Dr. Gary Roberts, know what they're talking about. They made sure that the book provided revelations and insights regarding political strife and the answers that could solve them.

Job Strategies for the 21st Century: How to Assist Today's College Students during Economic Turbulence provides practical solutions to the challenges that today's college students face when attempting to find employment in an unstable economy. This book is specially designed for frustrated parents, anxious students, bewildered professors and educators, and those who sincerely care for college graduates. Dr. Daryl Green and Mr. William Bailey offer an entertaining and delightful discussion to help your audience increase their chances for future employment.

Marketing for Professionals: The Handbook for Emerging Entrepreneurs in the 21st century provides a roadmap for steering clear of marketing landmines by focusing on market opportunities in a systematic fashion. This book doesn't waste readers' time with literary fluff but provides meaningful content to apply. Topics include marketing strategy, competition, new product deployment, marketing mix (product, price, place, and promotion), niche markets/segmentation, and marketing analyses to make a few key topics. Many marketing textbooks deal with marketing for traditional companies and organizations. However, few books narrow in on the needs of today's young entrepreneurs at heart. The purpose of this book is to provide hope in the midst of this uncertainty. Through this book, you will (a) examine obstacles ahead for emerging businesses, (b) learn relevant marketing concepts to grow your business, and (c) examine how to determine favorable market opportunities while staying ahead of your competitors.

More Than a Conqueror: Achieving Personal Fulfillment in Government Service, co-authored with wife Estraletta, provides a message about how to take positive steps in achieving your goals while in government service. However, many individuals will be able to benefit from this book. In More than a Conqueror, you will (a) go beyond your self-imposed limitation by breaking the barrier of your self-doubt and (b) protect and cultivate your life in order to bring forth the best you can in your generation.

My Cup Runneth Over: Setting Goals for Single Parents and Working Couples guides families in setting goals for themselves. Daryl and his wife have first-hand experience on this subject, both working full-time jobs and raising three active children. This book uses a new management process called Meshing™. The book is very different from most family books, focusing more on practical solutions. Daryl and his wife, Estraletta, have used their experience as managers in the government, non-profit, and private business sectors to assist families in this country to do what they have done- take control of their families. Written in an informal, entertaining style, it provides information to families that give them HOPE. Creatively illustrated with graphics and charts, the book is also indexed for quick reference. It is essential reading for families in search of a purpose. Special Awards: January Book of the Month, The Larry Young Show 1998, Special Black History Award at Atkins Library, Featured on Heaven 600 (The Top Gospel Radio Station in the Country).

Second Chance presents non-profit organizations with a way to use operations management tools to make them more efficient and better equipped to assist their clients and constituents in meeting their needs. Dr. Green co-authored with one of his students. Through the eyes of student Noriko Chapman, readers will be taken on a magical journey of overcoming a difficult situation in operations management and life.

Selling by Objectives provides insight into how to create more sales during an economic crisis using seven key ingredients. The book offers practical solutions that today's organizations can easily digest and implement even in an unstable economy. This book is essential not only for salespeople but also for any professional involved in selling goods and services with a desire to be successful in the marketplace. Non-profit organizations, business owners, college students, professors, entrepreneurs, and other sales organizations can benefit from this book.

Writing for Professionals provides individuals with authoritative writing tools. It offers strategies, practical guidelines, resources, and a host of suggestions to help with publishing goals. The advice in this book can be useful for a wide variety of professions, including business executives, teachers, scientists, engineers, attorneys, and many others.

Subject Virtue Index

G

H

I

P

S

APPENDIX 1

DR. D. GREEN STRATEGICPLANASDEAN (1ST 5 YEARS)

Dr. Daryl D. Green, Dean of Langston Business School

The Nehemiah Strategy: 5-Year Plan:

1. Year 1-2: Local Focus

- Conduct listening tour with all major stakeholders (students, faculty, alumni, advisory board, corporations, community groups, schools).
- Build a high performing team that is adapted to the 'Future of
- Build a Wishlist for students and faculty that will enhance the quality of the student learning experience.
- Promote the merit of the business school through innovative marketing strategies (i.e., media interviews, social media, written articles/editorials, podcast guests, community presentations and speeches).
- Conduct situational analysis of Langston Business School including core competencies, curriculum, and academic capacity.
- Establish strategic partnerships with other universities, chambers, businesses, local black churches, schools, and community organizations.

- Host community events and workshops to engage with local stakeholders.
- Collaborate with local minority-owned businesses and initiate mentorship programs.
- Conduct Innovation Bootcamp (AI, Branding, Culture Intelligence for All Current LU Students as Baseline.

2. Year 2-3: Regional Expansion
   - Extend outreach to regional HBCUs, fraternities/ sororities, and student associations.
   - Participate in regional conferences of black chambers of commerce.
   - Forge partnerships with regional corporations promoting diversity and inclusion.

3. Year 3-4: National Connections
   - Strengthen relationships with national organizations like the National Urban League and NAFEO.
   - Attend and present at national conferences, emphasizing Langston University's commitment to career readiness, global awareness, and inclusion (belonging, inclusion).
   - Seek partnerships with major national corporations with established diversity programs.

4. **Year 4-5: Corporate Partnerships**

- Deepen collaborations with Fortune 500 companies, fostering internship and job placement opportunities.
- Engage with the National Minority Supplier Development Council for potential corporate sponsorships.
- Establish Langston University as a hub for promoting diversity and inclusion in education and corporate sectors.

APPENDIX 2

DAILY READINGPLAN:365DAYSIN PROVERBS

Because Proverbs has 31 chapters, a simple way to soak in its wisdom all year is to read one proverb verse each day, cycling through a 31-day pattern each month. Below is a suggested 31- day cycle, each paired with a virtue. Use this table monthly for all 12 months (31 × 12 ≈ 365).

You can copy this table twelve times in Word (one for each month) or simply reuse it monthly.

DAY – SCRIPTURE – VIRTUE

1 - Proverbs 1:7 – Fear of the Lord

2 - Proverbs 2:6 – Wisdom

3 - Proverbs 3:5–6 – Trust

4 - Proverbs 4:7 – Pursuit of Wisdom

5 - Proverbs 5:21 – Accountability

6 - Proverbs 6:6–8 – Diligence

7 - Proverbs 7:2 – Obedience

8 - Proverbs 8:13 – Reverence and Holiness

9 - Proverbs 9:9 – Teachability

10 - Proverbs 10:9 – Integrity

11 - Proverbs 11:3 – Moral Guidance

12 - Proverbs 12:18 – Wise Speech

13 - Proverbs 13:20 – Mentoring & Companionship

14 - Proverbs 14:29 – Patience

15 - Proverbs 15:1 – Gentle Answers

16 - Proverbs 16:3 – Commitment of Plans

17 - Proverbs 16:9 – God's Direction

18 - Proverbs 16:24 – Gracious Words

19 - Proverbs 17:22 – Joyful Heart

20 - Proverbs 18:13 – Listening

21 - Proverbs 19:20 – Counsel

22 - Proverbs 20:5 – Deep Insight

23 - Proverbs 21:3 – Justice

24 - Proverbs 21:5 – Diligent Planning

25 - Proverbs 22:4 – Humility

26 - Proverbs 23:12 – Discipline

27 - Proverbs 24:10 – Courage in Crisis

28 - Proverbs 25:28 – Self-Control

29 - Proverbs 27:17 – Community & Collaboration

30 - Proverbs 28:20 – Faithfulness

31 - Proverbs 31:8–9 – Advocacy for the Voiceless

Repeat this cycle each month. Over the course of a year, you will have prayed through these key proverbs twelve times, allowing their wisdom to move from your eyes to your heart to your leadership decisions.

Walk By Faith Publishing | www.wbyf.site

www.linkedin.com/in/drdarylgreen/

@Dr.DarylGreen2014

@DrGreen2014

@Daryld.Green

@DrDarylGreen

www.ingramcontent.com/pod-product-compliance
Lightning Source LLC
LaVergne TN
LVHW010605110826
845149LV00003B/773

* 9 7 8 1 9 7 2 7 6 0 0 0 0 *